The Naked Truth

Also by Chunichi

A Gangster's Girl
Married to the Game
Girls From the Hood

The Naked Truth

Chunichi

URBAN BOOKS LLC

Dedication

This book is dedicated to the two strongest people in my life, my mother Angelia McZeek and my husband Aron "Belly" Campbell.

Urban Books
10 Brennan Place
Deer Park, NY 11729

ISBN 978-0-7394-7735-9

Printed in United States of America

This is a work of fiction. Any references or similarities to actual events, real people, living, or dead, or to real locals are intended to give the novel a sense of reality. Any similarity to other names, characters, places, and incidents is entirely coincidental.

ACKNOWLEDGMENTS

Like always, I would like to thank God first. The past year has been one heck of a roller coaster and without God I would have never reached the end of the ride. I had a lot of plans of my own, but they all crumbled because they weren't God's plans. And believe me, after all I've been through, I'm definitely listening now; while continuously praying for strength and guidance as I walk the path He has laid. God has truly blessed me with wonderful talent and given me the opportunity to touch so many.

To my literary family, thanks for your support. My agent Marc Gerald, you are the greatest! Thanks for being there no matter the time of day. To my co-agent and literary big sister, Nikki Turner, love you girl. Thanks for being a shoulder to cry on when I'm down, yet a stern agent when I'm slipping. I'm right behind you, girlie, following your lead.

To my new friends and true friends, thanks for having my back. Segeeta Bland, always 'bout those dollars baby! That's what's up! Keep up the good work. Stephanie Cook, still keeping it real. I'll have you no other way. Natasha Billingsly, you're more than just a friend and I hope to always have you by my side. Kim Todd, thanks for being the best assistant a chick could ask for. You are always on the job! Sophronia Plum, ain't nothing changed but the game and you are still the star player. Tracey Davis, Toya Smith, and Tiffany Duncan, thanks for being true. Your loyalty will never be forgotten. Chrissy Smith, continued success in all that you do. Lisa, Tomona and Tamara, hold down the fort and keep the Naughty Girls in line. Kisha, Melainie, and Chele you girls are still going strong. Your goals are in arms reach. I wish y'all the best. Miesha Camm, author of *Hidden Intentions*, great success now that you are part of the literary fam. Deneen Majors, Tasha and the whole Major Creations crew, it's great to be back home. Cee, I see you're still my biggest fan and still promoting. Thanks for being on the team. Dante' Davis, thanks for being my big brother at heart and watching over me. Jason, you're part of the fam now buddy, there's no turning back! Jamel aka laughy-laughy, your laughter alone brightens my day.

To my family, I love you all. To my mom, Angelia McZeek, you're one of a kind. Thanks for being by my side through the ups and downs and loving me the same no matter what. My little brother, Vincent McZeek, keep your eye on the prize and I got your back. To my in-laws in Jamaica, I couldn't ask for a better extended family. Thanks for welcoming me with open arms. Finally to my husband, although it has been a rough ride, we still pulled through. We've grown closer with each hurdle we jumped. I love you.

Finally with little respect, I give the middle finger to all you haters! I've discovered haters are not always that obvious. They come in all shapes and sizes posing as friends, family, associates, leaders and mentors; but eventually they show their true selves. All haters bow down!

PROLOGUE

I knew it wouldn't be long until I was back on top. It ain't no way they could hold a gangster bitch like me down! I've played every position there is, from hood rich to a stripping chick, and all in the name of the game. It's taken all I've had—sex, blood, and tears—but I'm finally back on my throne where the queen belongs.

Since I've moved to Atlanta, I've come into contact with a new breed of niggas and have even managed to cop myself one—an entertainer. And it wouldn't be worth speaking on if I wasn't indulging in all the benefits that come along with it. Not even Vegas—God rest his soul—could set me up like this dude has. The long-overdue extravagance that I'm being showered with is the treatment a true diva like me deserves. So to all those chicks back in VA, they can just look for me on *Cribs* and choke to death on their throw-up, 'cause I know they gonna be sick at the thought of me shitting on 'em!

The hundred grand I bucked Snake for was well worth it. He should have slept with both eyes open because, thanks to that money, I was able to get the clothes, crib, and attitude necessary to pull a true Atlanta baller. Unlike the small-time dealers in VA, Atlanta niggas do it real big! The CLK has been replaced with the CLS; gold fronts with iced-out grills; condos with million-dollar, high-rise penthouses. And the sexiest thing of all—Northern slang has been replaced with country grammar. Shit! Atlanta is definitely on a different level.

With that, and dough on my mind, I went to ATL in full effect, ready to grab the first thing balling. Big, tall, fat, or small, I wasn't discriminating, as long as his pockets were deep and his safe even deeper!

It didn't take long for me to peep out the competition and catch on to the game the chicks ran in the *A*. Just like the bitch we all hate, Super Head, the video chicken, or whatever they calling her these days, the shit is real! Chicks make it their business to get at these dudes and take them for a ride.

Off the top, I knew I had to come at the fellas from a different angle, so I took it back to the basics. No one in Atlanta knew my past, or anything about me, for that matter, so I could easily portray whatever image I wanted. I decided it was time to challenge myself, taking on a role that wasn't anything near the real me. So I decided to stun the academy with my Oscar-worthy performance of that of a good girl. What guy doesn't love the girl next door?.

THE NAKED TRUTH

No longer *A Gangster's Girl*, no longer *Married to the Game*, now it's Miss Prissy, bitches! But don't get it twisted and get caught up in the role I play, and take me for a stupid chick and try to fuck me . . . 'cause I could easily switch that shit up and make it *The Return of a Gangster's Girl!*

CHAPTER 1

Ceazia

"I'm bbbbbbaaaaacccckkkkk!"

With my mind on the prize, once I made my smooth landing in Atlanta, GA, it didn't take long for me to find my prey and hunt him down. This Georgia peach was preserved all the way from VA, and my juices were 100% concentrate!

In all honesty, I don't know if I actually hunted down my prey or if he carelessly just stumbled into my trap. Nonetheless, I ran into one of the hottest rappers on the charts, Parlay—Jason Williams to his family and the government.

It was barely even a month after I had settled down in my nice little condo in the Peachtree area, that I met Parlay the night of his album release party at Visions nightclub. All that Saturday morning and afternoon I groomed myself like the finest pedigree bitch I was. I hit one of the beauty shops, where I had my hair flat-ironed so straight that it made Pocahontas' hair look like Buckwheat's. The Koreans hooked my French manicure and pedicure up so tight that a bitch almost changed her name to Paris. The crimson pantsuit that I picked up at an upscale, second-hand boutique had been made for each curve on my body.

I know what you're thinking—*A second-hand shop*?

I know. I even surprised myself, but when I saw it hanging in the window, I knew this particular garment would receive justice the second time around. I was just fortunate enough that the first bitch came to her senses and realized that she had to give it up and allow its rightful owner to stake her claim.

I set the standard when I walked up into the club with the perfect pumps; rhinestones embedded in the ankle strap. One would have thought that I was the guest of honor, the way heads turned when I arrived at the event.

Folks automatically pegged me for being Parlay's girl, assuming, I guess, that someone of his caliber wouldn't be caught dead with anything but the shiniest trophy on the shelf.

It didn't take a rocket scientist to figure out where the man of the hour was. All I had to do was follow the trail of hair weave, silicon, and clear stiletto shoes; the groupies' calling card.

I positioned myself where I didn't necessarily have a clear view of him, but that wasn't what was important. With my back to him and his entourage, I ordered a drink from the bar. After receiving my drink, I slowly turned around on my stool. Looking down at my drink, I innocently, yet seductively, took a sip from the straw. I then slowly looked up, and just like I thought, his eyes were fixated on me.

Upon first glance, I knew I had him. It was something about the way he looked at me with those deep-set brown eyes that let me know what was up in a matter of seconds. Who cares if he did have his woman on his arm, and a few groupies to boot?

Instantly, I threw a seductive stare back. Once I hypnotized him with these panther eyes of mine, it was "game over." I knew at that moment Parlay would be mine to keep.

I took the black, long-strapped evening bag off my shoulder and pulled out Parlay's latest CD, which I had picked up at the record store after getting my hair done.

I took one more sip of my drink and then sat it back down on the bar before heading his way.

With my signature strut, the crowd seemed to disperse for me until I was situated in front of the table where Parlay was.

"Excuse me, Mr. Parlay?" I bat my eyes. "Could you autograph my CD for me, please?" I slid him the CD across the table and pulled a black Sharpie out of my purse.

His eyes said, "For you, baby, anything." He stuck his hand out and took the pen.

While he removed the cover label and began writing, I pushed the mute button on the tired-ass game the lames in his crew were trying to spit at me.

Parlay handed me my CD back.

"Thank you."

"Anytime."

I turned to walk away. *Hell, that's all he could say.* My ass had a tendency to make niggas speechless.

I made my way through the crowd.

"Hey," I heard him call.

I turned around.

Parlay held up my Sharpie. "You forgot your pen."

He reminded me of an old boyfriend who is all too thrilled, when he finds that the chick that just dropped his ass, left something of hers in his apartment—he can't wait to call her to tell her to come pick it up so that he can see her one more time, in hopes of having some break-up finale sex.

"That's all right. You keep it. You never know who else might want your autograph too." I winked and then I stepped.

As I exited the club I looked down at the CD Parlay had signed. I couldn't keep the smile secured behind my pouty lips, as it stretched across my face. I had to pat myself on the back for that one. In record time, I had done what all those 'ho's would spend all night trying to do—I had gotten Parlay to personalize my CD with both his autograph *and* cell phone number.

Becoming a Georgia peach took a little changing, but once I realized exactly what advantages those changes had, I was fully willing. I guess the shortage of straight men and excess of strip clubs had turned all the girls bisexual, so being slightly straight made me a part of the minority. Luckily, I was a freak in the bed and willing to explore just about anything for the love of money; otherwise, I may have ended up with the short end of the stick.

I learned that many men in Atlanta assumed bisexuality to be just simply part of life. The ones I came across seemed quite disappointed to hear that I didn't get down like that. So when it came to Parlay, I took no chances. When he expressed his fantasy to me of having another chick join us in bed, I quickly delivered.

Parlay's birthday, June 15th, was right around the corner, and I couldn't think of a more perfect gift.

Of course, I lied and I told him that it would be a first for me, but I assured him he wouldn't be disappointed. Banking on the one experience I had in Cancun, along with instructions from a wide collection of lesbo porno to make me a pro, I planned to deliver Parlay a threesome he would never forget!

I scouted Atlanta for the hottest chicks the city had to offer, from The Gentlemen's Club to Magic City. And I must say, I was pretty impressed when I finally found her. Diamond was her name, and she was flawless in every aspect. Not only was she attractive on the outside, she was just as beautiful inside. She stood five feet, eight inches, and had a small waist. Her skin was a cocoa-brown with red undertones. I loved her jet-black hair, which had deep waves all the way down her back. And it didn't hurt that she had a perfect white smile to add to her sex appeal.

Diamond, like most of the perspective candidates I had in mind, was a dancer too, but not the same type as the other girls. A creative art graduate from Georgia State

University, she spent her days working at her very own dance school created for the city youth. And to top it all off, she was a Scorpio just like me, sharing the same sexual appetite, along with many other things. It just doesn't get any better. There was not one bad thing any man or woman could say about that gorgeous little Indian girl.

I met Diamond unexpectedly. Although I was searching for the perfect woman to bring home to Parlay, Diamond just fell in my lap, literally. I was on one of my weekly shopping sprees at my favorite stores, Neiman Marcus, in Lenox Mall. As I sat trying on a pair of snakeskin Versace sandals, I noticed a young lady staring from afar.

At first, I thought to myself, *What the fuck is this chick staring at?* But the more I observed, the more I realized what was going on.

Like I said before—it's all in the eyes. And her eyes were saying, "I want you."

I smiled and turned my attention back toward the several pair of shoes I had in front of me.

Seemingly starving for attention, the young lady came over. "Those shoes really look nice on you." She stood over me.

"Thanks," I said, rather short.

Diamond was determined to force a conversation out of me. "Wow! That heel is high. I don't think I could even walk in those."

"Oh, it's not hard at all. It's only a three-and-a-half-inch heel." I looked down at the shoe and then slid it off my foot, as though I was Cinderella with the glass slipper.

"Here"—I handed her the sandals—"Why don't you try it?"

She sat down in the chair next to me and placed the shoes on her feet. "Perfect fit."

She stood up and took a couple of steps then stumbled and fell directly into my lap. "Told ya!" she laughed hysterically.

While still sitting on my lap, she continued to chat. "My name is Diamond. And you are?" She extended her hand.

"I'm Ceazia. It's nice to meet you, Diamond." I gave her a small shove as an indication to get off my lap.

"Oh, I was so comfortable here." She stood up and removed the shoes from her feet. "I almost forgot we were in a department store." Diamond gave me the same seductive stare as before, as she handed me the shoes.

That was enough confirmation for me. From there I knew she would be the perfect candidate to take home to Parlay.

I watched the shoes dangle in front of me before I took them from her hand and placed them back in the box. "Well, Diamond, it was nice chatting with you," I said, gathering the shoes I wanted to purchase. I then walked away.

"You all set, ma'am?" the salesman who had gotten all the shoes for me asked.

I nodded and proceeded to follow him to the register.

Diamond walked behind, fishing in her purse for something. Just as I made it to the register, she handed me a business card.

I looked down at it—ATLANTA BEAUTIES, INC. Although I wasn't familiar with that company, from looking at Diamond, I just assumed she was some sort of model.

"Can't wait to hear from you," Diamond said with confidence, before walking off.

Like a dude, I found myself watching her hips sway back and forth, butt bouncing with every step. I just shook my head and proceeded to check out at the register, knowing damn well that she had every reason to be as confident as she was, because I had every intention on ringing her phone.

"May I speak to Diamond?" I spoke through the phone receiver.

"Speaking."

"Hi, Diamond. This is Ce—"

"Yes, Ceazia." She cut me off, letting me know that she knew exactly who I was.

I was impressed, but didn't let on. "How are you today?"

"Better now," Diamond said.

I could hear her smile over the phone. "Same here."

I decided to go ahead and play along. "So, Diamond, I have a little bit of running around I have to do today and I was just wondering . . ."

"I'd love to—Is two o'clock fine?"

I took the phone away from my ear and just stared at it. *Can you believe this bitch?* She thought she really did have me pegged. I chuckled and put the phone back to my ear.

We agreed to meet for lunch at two o'clock that afternoon.

I arrived at the restaurant at two o'clock sharp to find an even more prompt Diamond already seated and sipping on an iced tea.

After our pleasantries, I quizzed her on a few things, just to see where her head was. I wasn't trying to bring just any old chick into my man's home.

I was impressed to learn she was a creative arts graduate from Georgia State University and spent a lot of time conducting free dance classes at the local youth centers. Her goal was to eventually open a dance studio of her own.

I shared a thing or two about myself; the "good girl" side anyway. I mentioned my relationship with Parlay. Cluing her in on the fact that I wasn't straight lesbo didn't seem to deter her interest in me, at least not enough not to land me a second lunch date.

After a few more meetings with Diamond, I was pleased, and convinced that she was the one. Although a tender twenty-one, Diamond seemed to have a lot going for her, enough where it wouldn't be in her complete best interest to go run and tell of her personal escapades with a well-known celebrity.

Whether it was lunch, a movie, dinner, or just hanging out at her place, I was more and more impressed at each of our meetings.

Finally, as we sat on the couch in my condo, the time came for me to proposition her.

From the photo albums I had flipped through while at

her place, I figured she wasn't a stranger to the dick because I had seen her hugged up with a guy or two, but to my surprise, her response to my proposition was just the opposite of what I had expected.

"Look, Ceazia," Diamond said, placing her hand on top of mine, "I really like you. And I love a girl who is into pleasing her mate. But the thing is, I really like you, not your mate. I'm sure Parlay is a really nice lay—and it's not that I'm trying to be with you on the side on anything—but if I am going to be with you, I don't want any added interruptions."

She stroked my hair and leaned in closer, going for the kiss.

Fuck. I had to think quick on my feet to not allow her to flip the script on something that was my production.

As her soft lips touched mine, I sat there waiting for her next move, which was that of her tongue separating my lips.

I pulled back shyly. "Diamond," I whispered.

"You okay?"

I could hear the concern in her voice.

"Yes, it's just that . . ." I paused for theatrics. "I—"

"Shhh." She placed her index finger on my lips. "You don't have to say it; I can see it in your eyes. You've never been with a woman before, Ceazia, have you?"

I didn't mind allowing her to feel like the elder in the relationship, as long as in the end I got what I wanted. I slowly lowered my head, as if embarrassed by my lack of experience.

"I'm sorry if I led you to believe that. It's just that

when I saw you, I was so intrigued by you. I had never felt that way before about a . . ."

"A girl," Diamond answered for me.

"No, a woman."

On that note, I know her pussy got wet. I continued, while I had her juices good and flowing. "I guess me asking you to be with me and my boyfriend is because I was just scared to be with you alone. I mean, I'm older than you and everything. I didn't want to disappoint you, and I figured, if I froze up or anything, I could use Parlay to run interference."

Bitches weren't any different than men, when it all came down to it—Allow them to feel dominant in the relationship, provide that "needy" factor, and they are putty in the palm of your hands.

After hearing me out and then taking a minute to allow my words to sink in, Diamond finally spoke. "I hear what you're saying, but I really want it to be all about you—just me and you."

"I really want to be with you too, but I would just feel much more comfortable if we did a threesome. I know I'm being selfish, but at the same time, I wouldn't feel as though I'm cheating on Parlay."

If it wasn't for the fact that I needed to continue to look appealing in Diamond's eyes, I would have let the tear that welled up in my eye to fall. But no way was I going to fuck up the perfection of my eyeliner that highlighted my eyes and end up looking like Tammy Faye Baker. My eyes spoke more than my mouth ever could.

Diamond sighed. "I want you to be comfortable. And I guess we could look at this as sort of a tester; we each get to sample before we sit down to a full-course meal with each other."

I could have been opening up a can of worms, but what the hell, I was into this role way too deep.

"But what if you don't like the sample, and I never get a full taste of you?" I licked my lips.

"Don't worry, that's not going to happen. I just want to make you happy."

"Well, I'm glad you're into making me happy, but what would really be pleasing to me is seeing Parlay sex you from behind while your head is buried in my lap."

"But I really wanted it to be all about you," Diamond whined. "I want to please you."

"Well, you make sure I'm pleased, baby girl," I said, allowing a little bit of my feistiness to find its way out, "and I'll gladly return the favor."

The grin on her face told me I had sung music to her ears. "That's exactly what I wanted to hear, baby. You won't be disappointed."

Easily manipulated, Diamond agreed to the threesome with Parlay, with the misconception that eventually it would be all about me and her. Little did she know, I was willing to go to the highest extremes, from a grand stack to jewels, if necessary; there was no limit when it came to pleasing my man.

CHAPTER 2

Danielle

"Playing the game my way"

Another day, another dick, I thought to myself as I brushed my teeth and watched Dario through the bathroom mirror. He lay on the bed like a lump on a log.

Sex with him was never a thrill, but it kept my position as next candidate for partnership with the law firm secure. For each day I had to relive this tortuous act with Dario, I added another kick to Ceazia's ass. She was the reason why I was in this predicament in the first place. And little did she know, the day I got the chance, I was gonna make sure she relived every miserable moment I had to deal with since Snake's death.

After Snake's death, a life of hell would have been a step-up for me. But knowing that everything happens for a reason, that dominos fall in line in order to lay that last one flat, and every dot connects in order to make a vivid picture, the series of devastation I endured was supposed to land me in the town I was in today, leaving crab-ass Virginia behind.

Once relocating to the ATL, I landed a job with one of Atlanta's biggest law firms: Johnson, Smith, Davis and Williams. And after getting this job by any means, and I do mean any, as in "whatever it took," I needed to be the next partner.

The one way to secure that position—lock one of the senior partners, Dario Duncan, between my legs.

Fat, black and ashy, and topped off with a small penis, Dario had nothing to give me even the slightest thrill! But one thing I'd learned from the drama with Snake was that sex secures any woman's needs or wants, as long as it was with the right person. The one that can create results for all of your heartache and troubles—and that Dario was.

Not quite Mr. Right, but definitely Mr. Right Person. Shit, I would much rather masturbate to a DVD from my extensive porno collection than have sex with Dario, but a chick's gotta do what a chick's gotta do!

Wearing the *her* portion of the thick, white, his-and-her English cotton bathrobe set, I walked into the luxurious master bathroom, which Dario had decorated in an earth tone and stone décor. I untied the belt, opened the robe, and let it slide down my shoulders and onto the floor. I took three steps up into the completely tiled two-head shower that was the size of a walk-in closet. I walked over to the showerhead on the left side and turned the water temperature on hell. I then walked over to the showerhead on the right and did the same thing.

Steam immediately filled the space.

I stood in the middle of the shower, allowing the water

shooting from both directions to assault my body, begging Calgon to take me away.

"DDDDaaaaaaarrrrriiiiiooooo," I sang from the bathroom shower to Dario, still asleep in bed when I had gone to take a shower.

I imagined him grunting as he rolled his fat ass over, pulling the covers over his face as he did each morning after we had one of these sickening rendezvous.

My stomach turned as I thought about the sex we had the previous night. *An hour of foreplay for a minute of play—The things you gotta do to stay on top.*

With his small pecker, I had to do a whole lot of work. I laughed aloud as I lathered my loofa with shea butter body wash.

"Big daddddyyyyyy!" I called him again, using my sex kitten appeal to lure him from a deep sleep into my gauntlet.

I figured the sooner he woke up, the sooner he could get his Jenny Craig-dropout ass up and dressed, and I could be on my merry way. Waking up to find me gone wasn't how Dario preferred things; me either, for that matter. I learned early that it was better that I stay and offer a formal goodbye versus that nigga calling me and whining all day how he didn't get a chance to tell me goodbye, and how he wanted to hook back up for a more cordial farewell. YUCK! It was better to give him that small bit of comfort than to have the threat of having to fuck him any sooner than I needed to.

After I called out to him once again, Dario finally raised his naked body from the dead.

With nothing but rolls of fat on his body, not having the strength the night before to slip on anything to sleep in after falling out exhausted from the "one-hour-and-one-minute" workout, he entered the bathroom looking like a yawning hippo, wobbling his way toward the shower.

"Hey, sweetheart." he said as he headed in the opposite direction of the shower to go use the toilet.

"Hey to you."

After using the bathroom he washed his hands and walked over to the shower.

I leaned my head out.

He kissed me on my cheek. "What's up?"

"Nothing, baby." I stepped back into the shower. "I'm just taking a shower so I can get dressed and get ready to go, but I didn't want to leave without saying goodbye." I tried to give him a subtle hint.

He hopped in the shower without hesitation and quickly found my body that was buried in the steam. I tried to wash up as quickly as possible, because I didn't want to take the chance of him getting a hard-on and wanting more sex. I didn't feel my stomach could bear another episode.

Apparently I didn't move fast enough, because just as I turned around to rinse my face, I felt a brush across my back. At first I ignored it, hoping it was just his fat stomach brushing against my back, but it didn't take long for me to realize it was his hand.

He gently applied pressure on my back as an indication he wanted me to bend over.

Even though that was the best option—I wouldn't have

to look at this whale of a man—I just wasn't up for it. Besides, this nigga didn't even have a condom on, and the last thing I needed was the disgusting feeling of his nut running all up inside of me.

"No, Dario, you don't have a condom, baby," I said in my best baby girl voice.

"You can't leave me like this, Danielle," he begged.

I knew he wouldn't give up without a fight.

I didn't have the time or patience to go back and forth with him, so I closed my eyes and did what I had to do. I got down on my knees and gave him the blowjob of a lifetime.

I never gave them lazy-ass blowjobs that sometimes defeated the purpose of not fucking a nigga in the first place. If you don't give it your all, he might not come and you'll end up having to spread them legs anyway, just so that he can hurry up and get *his*. Now you've ended up sucking his dick and fucking him. So if I was gonna do that shit, then I was gonna do it right.

I took Dario by his hard limb and placed it in my mouth. I paused and allowed it to just lie on my tongue, my lips wrapped around it, allowing just the warmth of my mouth alone to stimulate him.

Slowly, I began going back and forth on him. As hard as I tried to do it Vanessa Del Rio style, I was gagging with every stroke.

Amazingly, that turned this guy on.

"Deep throat this big dick, baby," he mumbled between groans. "That's right—choke on this big dick."

Little did he know, if I had to, I could swallow his little

dick whole. The gags were not a reflex from a long dick, but rather a reflex from a disgusting act—I wanted to vomit the entire time.

Lucky for me, not only was he fat, disgusting, and poor in bed, he also was a "minute" man.

Two minutes later, my job was over.

I quickly washed up and jumped out the shower.

In ten minutes flat, I was dressed and out the door. I wasn't wasting any more time. I had to get the hell away from him, before I found myself having to let him hit it from the back after all.

Once I was in my car, a nice little fully loaded Eclipse, I headed straight to the interstate. That was the quickest route away from Dario.

After a couple of miles, good and far away from his ass, I pulled out my cell phone and called up Richard, my fiancé.

"Hi, baby!" I yelled into the phone with excitement.

"What's up, baby?" He responded with just as much enthusiasm.

I had met Richard shortly after my move to Atlanta. His lawyer just happened to be one of the senior partners of the firm I worked for. One day as I headed out for lunch, Richard was on his way in to speak with his attorney. Our eyes locked at first glance. Once I realized that I was staring at him and that he had caught me staring, I put my head down in complete embarrassment. But then I thought to myself, *Hell, he's staring at me too.*

"Hey, sexy," he asked with a nod, "what kind of trouble could a sweet-looking girl like you possibly be in where you need the services of this place?"

I smiled. "I'm not in any trouble. I usually am trouble."

"I see," he said with the sexiest smile ever spread across his lips. "Well, Trouble—"

"Danielle."

"Excuse me?"

"Danielle," I repeated. "The name is Danielle, not Trouble."

"Ummm, Danielle." He extended his hand. "I'm Richard, Danielle, but like I was saying, if you ever want to get into some trouble with me"—He handed me a card from the wallet he retrieved out of his pants pocket—"just holler at me."

I took the card and headed on out to lunch. Needless to say, once I got off work, went home, took me a shower and got relaxed, I called his ass, quick fast and in a hurry. And the rest, as they say, is history. From that day forth that six-six, 200-pound caramel frame was mine to keep. There was no way I could walk away from that gorgeous, baby face, accented with a beautiful white smile, dimples, and black curly hair.

Richard was my baby, and I loved him to death, but he was always on the road. Because he played for the NBA, nearly six months out of the year was spent away from home, and the other six months was split 50-50, quality time with me, hangout time with the boys.

I hated being apart from him, but I knew as an NBA wife

I had to learn to live with him not being home as well as deal with the boys, groupies, whores, and even the down-low athletes that I'd heard so much about.

"When am I going to see you?"

"Hopefully I can come through one day this week, baby. You miss me?"

"Yes, I do, and I want my man home with me."

"Man, don't start that shit, Danny. You already know how it is. Like I've told you before, as my wife, this is the shit you're going to have to deal with. This is my life, so speak now or forever hold your piece. And don't hold that shit in until the preacher asks you at the altar."

Damn! I guess he told me.

That pretty much ended the conversation—whatever the king says, goes. Birth date July 18th, Richard was borderline Cancer and Leo, and it was times like these when the king lion roared.

I sucked it up and accepted his word. "I'm sorry, baby. Just know that I miss you. Have a good game tonight. I love you."

"Love you too," Richard responded, before ending the call.

I flipped the phone closed and placed it down in my purse.

Five minutes hadn't passed before my phone rang again.

It's Richard. He's called to apologize for coming off like that before. I fumbled through my Marc Jacob bag, trying to get to my phone. *He does manage to come to his senses every now and then.*

I looked down at the caller ID, and to my disappointment it wasn't Richard. It was Jonathan, a young man I'd met one day while sipping a frappachino at Starbucks. He was sort of the "metrosexual" type. Not really my style, but I figured his position, a buyer for Chanel, would have great benefits. So without hesitation, I put him on my team.

"Hello," I said in a singsong voice.

My face brightened as I answered the phone. Jonathan always seemed to cheer up my day. He always said the right words and called at the right times. If only Richard had those same qualities.

"Hello, beautiful. How's your day going?" Jonathan asked, always concerned about my well-being.

"It's going okay. I just spoke to Richard. He upset me a little, but I'm fine now."

I was always open with any guy on my team that's part of the starting line-up. I made sure to let each one of them know up front about the star player that I'm on the sideline cheering for. That way, each one is aware of his position and can play it accordingly; even if it means he has to be benched momentarily.

Jonathan was especially understanding. He and I had a perfect arrangement. He was married to his wife, and I was "married to the game." He understood the rules perfectly—no feelings, no questions, just here to please each other—physical pleasure for him and financial and material pleasures for me—Who could ask for a better arrangement?

"How about brunch?" Jonathan offered.

" 'Brunch'?" I looked at my car's digital clock. My morning had been so hectic that I hadn't even thought twice about eating. "Sure. Where would you like to meet?"

We decided to meet at a delicatessen in the Buckhead area of Atlanta. Since I was already en route, it took me little time to get there.

As I arrived at the restaurant a few minutes earlier than Jonathan, I decided to take a seat and check my home voice mail.

"You have three new messages," the automated recording said.

"Hmmm, three calls," I said to myself, anxious to know who had called me.

My eagerness soon turned to dismay after the first two messages—Only bill collectors—Ms. Stevens owes this, and Ms. Stevens owes that.

I deleted the messages as soon as I heard, "This is Mr. Smith with County Financial," and "This is Miss So-and-So with such-and-such."

Once I reached the third message, my finger was already set on the number three to delete the message, but when I heard the familiar raspy voice of Shawn, I nearly dropped the phone.

"What up, sexy?" His words climbed out of the receiver and right into my ear, sending a chill down my spine. "This is Shawn—you know you ain't have to buck on me like that. I'm home and can't wait to reclaim my money and my kitty cat. Holla at a nigga 917-222—"

My body froze in a panic as my brain raced.

What the hell is Shawn doing home? I thought he would never get out. What about Richard? What if he finds out I set him up? What if he already knows and is setting me up? What am I going to do?

Shawn was Snake's New York drug connection. Shawn had a supplier in every aspect of the game—Jamaicans for weed, Colombians for coke, and even a few white boys for the X pills (Ecstasy).

After Snake died, Shawn and I had an arrangement. Basically, he kept me on a status that I was accustomed to, and in exchange, I kept him happy sexually. In the beginning, I felt extreme guilt and planned to renege on me and Shawn's little agreement, but Shawn had plans of his own.

After a few weeks, he became possessive and abusive, totally violating all the rules of the arrangement. With no way out and tired of the obligation, the beatings, and being dependent upon him, I made a vow to get him, as well as that bitch, Ceazia, the true cause of all my misery.

I continued to play along with Shawn's little game, as I executed a game of my own.

A few phone calls and a few months later, I was successful in setting Shawn up. I'd finally gotten him off my back. He was served with ten indictments, which resulted in a sentence of twenty years federal time. He went straight to jail.

With no get-out-of-jail-free card in sight, my job was finally done.

After completing my job with Shawn, my next objective was to serve Ceazia.

That Ceazia bitch had gotten away for the last time.

As soon as I had gotten word that she had fled to Atlanta after her personal murder spree, my shit was packed and I was on my way right behind her. I promised to serve her for each lick I had received, each dollar I had lost, and for each person she had killed. And that was a sentence much longer than any man behind bars had ever served.

Finally free from Shawn, I set out on a new beginning. It was time to put my law degree and parents' high-class status to work. Without hesitation, I moved out of Virginia and into Atlanta, leaving no trail. I just had no idea that fool, Shawn, would get out and track me down.

"Sorry to keep you waiting," Jonathan said softly in my ear, nearly scaring me half to death.

"Oh shit!" I screamed and held my chest. I thought I was going to have a massive heart attack. I didn't think my heart could take too many more surprises.

"I'm sorry. Did I startle you?" Jonathan asked.

"No. It's okay. I was just deep in thought and didn't even notice you coming behind me." I paced my breathing, trying to calm my nerves.

During the entire time at lunch, I found myself off in a daze. That message from Shawn really had my head screwed up. I mean, I swear on everything, I could hear that nigga's voice as if he was just right over my shoulder.

"Danielle . . . Danielle . . . Danielle," Jonathan called

out to me. "Danielle," I heard my name being called. "Danielle." It was getting louder. "Danielle!"

I swear I thought it was Shawn calling me. It took a moment, but then the voice finally registered in my mind.

By the time I answered him, I could tell he was pretty annoyed at my inattentiveness. "I'm sorry." I sighed and ran my hand down my forehead. "Baby, I have a lot on my mind, you know, with the big case coming up and all. One mess-up and it could ruin my chances for partner," I lied, quickly apologizing.

I had to be careful never to get Jonathan upset. Unlike the others, I knew he would leave my ass at any time if I got out of line. And I definitely wasn't trying to take the risk of losing his top-notch dick.

"I can tell there is something bothering you, sweetheart. If you like, I will excuse you from lunch early."

I accepted, but agreed to make it up to him later. He knew I would do exactly that too.

He paid the waiter, walked me to my car, and kissed me goodbye. His kiss alone made my body steam with lust. Jonathan knew the effect a simple touch could have on me.

"Why don't you come over to the condo and let me give you a nice massage?" He opened the car door for me, allowing me to slide into the driver's seat. He knew I would never pass on such an offer.

"Okay, baby, but no sex."

"No sex." He winked and then headed over to his white Jaguar.

He started his car and headed out of the parking lot, with me close on his bumper.

Twenty minutes later, we arrived at his Alpharetta condo. It wasn't where he lived; it was where we played. Jonathan rented a condo just for our secret rendezvous. Since we each had a significant other, we both had a lot to lose and couldn't risk the chance of getting caught red-handed at some hotel.

From the jump we both agreed to never jeopardize losing our mates by getting caught having sexual acts in either of our homes. With that said, our secret lover's pad was more than a worthy investment.

With limited time ahead of us, we wasted no time getting down to business. One glass of champagne and one body massage later, I found myself engaged in passionate sex. Too busy thrusting in and out of me like a slivering snake, Jonathan didn't have time for any "I-told-you-so's." He made love to me like a chef preparing a delicacy for the Queen.

Sex was always good with Jonathan, but something about this time seemed much different. The way he caressed me and kissed me was so warming and pleasant, but yet it all seemed so unusual.

After forty-five long minutes and multiple orgasms for me, Jonathan finally reached his peak. "I love you, Danielle," he moaned as he thrust himself deep inside me, forcing out the words through clenched teeth as he ejaculated.

Again, I found my body in a state of panic. I was lost for

words. And again, I felt like I was going to have a heart attack.

Jonathan sighed with gratification and rolled off of me.

I grabbed my chest and tried to pace my breathing, without making it look too obvious.

Luckily for me, Jonathan's phone rang. "Hello," he answered after reaching over and grabbing his phone off of the end table. "Just a minute, sweetie," he said to me. He got up out of the bed and walked his naked body into another room for privacy.

That was my indication that it was his wife on the phone. I could hear him lie to her as he explained to her how he was with a client.

I actually found myself getting a little jealous, the longer their conversation went on. I quickly got dressed and began to gather my things. I headed toward the door, clearing my throat just loud enough for him to hear, but not his wife on the other end of the phone.

I then walked past Jonathan, in an attempt to get his attention and rush him off the phone.

Evidently it worked, because a few moments later, he walked behind me and grabbed me around the waist. "You're so cute when you're jealous," he whispered in my ear and then kissed my neck.

"Who's jealous?" I responded sassily and headed out the door.

Jonathan rushed to throw on his boxers. I then heard him run up closely behind me, to make sure that I got to my car safely.

Once I reached the car, he gave me a small peck. "Goodbye."

I hopped in my car and drove off, admiring his sexy frame from a distance. Sure, I played my position allowing his wife to win this time, but one thing was for sure—hearing those three special words was a definite sign that my position would soon be changing to first string! So pad up, wifey. I'm hitting hard next game!

CHAPTER 3

Angel

"Caught in the act"

One thing I hate is when a nigga tries to play me. I knew it wouldn't be long before I caught John's cheating ass. I'd been tracking his cell phone calls for the past two months and following him for the past two weeks. It took nothing for me to trap his careless ass. After only a quick glance at his cell phone bill, it was obvious who the other woman was. There was only one other number that appeared on his bill as often as mine, and that he had conversations with that were as long as the ones he had with me. I knew the number had to belong to her!

John wasn't big on phone chatting, so when I saw repeated calls to another number and conversations up to forty-five minutes long, I knew what the deal was off the top.

Once I had the number, I used my connections and did a skip trace to get all of his little mistress's information. I got not only her home address but her work address, and even as much as her parents' name and address as well. I could have went and tracked the bitch down as soon as I collected all that information on her ass, but I wanted to be sure.

Thanks to that little bit of denial I had inside, I was pushed to investigate even further. And that's when I decided to follow John's little, sneaky ass. And like the dummy he was, he led me right to her! Only a man would be so damn stupid.

Like they say, the proof is in the pudding, and I had finally tasted more pudding than Bill Cosby. I watched as John and his tall, slim, label-'ho' walked into a small condo in a quiet and secluded part of town. It was as though I could feel fumes rising from my head as I watched John put the key into the door. I could only wonder if he purchased this secret spot for this exact purpose.

I paced my time perfectly; aiming to call his phone right in the middle of the act. I calculated the time it would take him to be right in the middle of a heated sexual moment based on our sexual routine. I called his cell phone after forty-five minutes, expecting to hear panting or to get no answer at all. I could only imagine what he would say and how he would act in front of that home-wrecking bitch he was with.

"Hello," John answered promptly.

He'd passed the first test. He answered the phone right away and was as relaxed as a sleeping baby.

"Hi, baby," I said, trying to sound excited to hear his voice.

"Hey, sweetie. What's up?"

"Nothing at all. I just was thinking about you and wanted to hear your voice. How's work?" I continued with small talk, just to see how long he would chat. I figured it was only a matter of time before Miss Thing would do something like cough, or clear her throat, or something loud enough to make her presence known.

"Work is fine, baby. Actually, I'm with a client right now."

That bitch was hardly a client. "Oh, I'm sorry. You should have said that in the beginning. Normally you don't even answer when you're in the middle of a meeting," I said, putting him out there.

"Well, this is sort of a casual client. He understands how it is when the wifey calls," he said with a little giggle.

"Oh, okay. Well go ahead, baby. Handle your business. I'll call you later."

"All right, baby," he was all too quick to say.

"Love you!" I yelled, just to see how he would respond to that one.

"I love you too, Angel," he stated before ending the call.

I was surprised how easy our conversation went. It made me wonder how many times I'd called before and he was actually with her. That chick was one of those 'ho's that knew how to play her position; never making a sound in the background, smiling in the wife's face, and keeping everything on the down low.

It looked as though John's little friend had gotten a little frustrated with his phone call, because not even five minutes after I hung up, she came prancing out the front door. A few seconds later, he came rushing behind her, with nothing on but a pair of boxers. That, of course, confirmed that they had just finished having sex. I guess I was just a few minutes too late with my call.

I could have very easily stepped out of my *her* Jag, which matched Jonathan's *his*, in my four-inch stiletto pumps with matching bag, which housed my nine, and let both the female and the man whore take one in the dome. But I just sat in the car with my flaming red nail polish that matched the flames that were brewing out of my nostrils, and continued to watch as John grabbed her from behind, placed his arms around her waist, and walked her to her car.

It took all I had not to run my car right into the both of them as they sat in her car kissing. They had no idea I was even watching, just like she had no idea I was following her ass right now.

My first instinct was to get out the car at the first red light we get to and confront her trifling ass, but I was trying to stay in my right mind. I didn't want to make any rash decisions that I'd regret later. But the longer I drove behind her, the more it set in.

My husband of ten years, Jonathan Powell, is having an affair. The same man that had nothing more than a high-school diploma and four years in the service under his belt when we first met. I practically made him! I gave him style; I gave him charm; I pointed him in the right direction. And now that he finally has a ground to stand on, he wants to be the king of the hill and send me tumbling down the side like a worthless little Jill.

My anger soon turned into pain. Tears began to blur my vision as I drove. Just as I was about to turn off and head home, the young scandalous 'ho' turned into a parking garage designated for Atlantic Station Lofts. Although this was not the address attached to her name when I did my detective work, this had to be where she lived.

Jackpot! I was pleased. This was the first step in planning my ultimate revenge.

Just as this little hussy had come into my life and torn it to pieces, I planned to do the same to her; but at an unbelievable magnitude. Once I was done with her, everything she touches will turn to shit. Although she thought she had it good, she'd soon realize she just entered the gates of Hell and that I was the fallen angel. But later for her; now it was time to deal with my unfaithful husband.

I rushed home, sure to beat John there. I figured, or at least hoped, he'd take a shower and wash any traces of the other women off of him.

Once inside, I changed clothes then pulled out the cleaning supplies. I cleaned the house from top to bottom then began to cook John's favorite meal—steamed fish and vegetables with my homemade jerk lemon and ginger sauce. It was a quick and easy dish to prepare, one he'd fallen in love with while on our honeymoon in Montego Bay.

Taking note of the time, I knew it wouldn't be long before he arrived. I dimmed all the lights, lit the fireplace, turned on the new Kem CD, and filled the Jacuzzi with hot water.

Five minutes later, John walked through the front door. "Wow! It smells great in here. What did I do to deserve this?" He walked into my arms and hugged me tightly.

"Nothing at all, honey. It's just a small token of my appreciation for you being such a great husband." I lied through my teeth, the same way he had done earlier on the phone with me. "You're always catering to me, so I figured that it was time I repay you. This is just the beginning." I took his coat and led him to the Jacuzzi.

He looked around at the spa-like atmosphere. "Baby, you appreciate me that much?"

I couldn't get that one itty-bitty lie out, so I just nodded and smiled.

As John took his clothes off and relaxed in the Jacuzzi, I set the candlelit table. After adding a few final touches, the table was perfect. The food had a fresh steam, and there was just enough lighting to create a romantic ambiance.

I poured us a glass of Pinot to top things off. I then went and met John at the Jacuzzi, where I stood with nothing but a towel in one hand and his silk pajama pants in the other. He needed nothing more.

"Here you are, sweetie." I handed him the towel.

I admired his body as he stepped out the Jacuzzi. It was as though he moved in slow motion, taking one foot out the tub at a time. The beads of water glistened off his creamy, black skin.

I then watched as he dried every inch of his frame. His body was flawless. John stood a perfect six feet, with every curve and cut in all the right places. I took a deep breath as the thought of that scandalous bitch caressing his perfect body flashed before me. I had to keep cool.

"Let's eat, honey." I handed him his pajama pants. "I

cooked your favorite," I said, trying to keep my mind focused elsewhere.

A huge smile crept across his face as he took the pants and slid them up to his waist. He knew exactly what his favorite was. John grabbed his robe that was hanging on the bathroom door and threw it on. I suppose he must have felt a chill or something, and nine times out of ten, it was from me in my desperate attempts to keep cool. He tied it loosely and then followed my lead.

I pulled his chair out for him as we approached the dining table. I walked over and uncovered the main course.

John's faced brightened. "Umm, umm, umm. Steamed fish. This truly is royal treatment. If I didn't know any better, I'd think this was our anniversary," he said, admiring the table set-up.

After I prepared his plate, I sat down next to him, without preparing a plate for myself. I picked up his fork and cut a piece of fish from his plate. I then placed it in front of his lying lips.

He smiled and slowly opened his mouth and took it all in. John was able to indulge in an entire meal without ever having to lift a finger. Bite by bite, I placed the contents of his plate in his mouth, looking directly in his eyes and giving him my most seductive smile. This smile held back all the tears and pain I felt inside as I realized my husband had no conscience.

An evil bitch would have cooked a killer stew for his ass, but not me. I aimed to kill him with kindness; it was his little bitch that had to worry.

I was treating him like the king of a palace that was built on my sweat, blood, and tears. As I noticed that he hadn't the least bit of guilt or regret in his eyes, those feelings of "death by kindness" began to change. I felt myself beginning to become angry. Again, I needed to channel my attention in a different direction before I fucked things up, so I decided to move to the bedroom.

"I hope you didn't get too full." I took the napkin and wiped John's mouth after feeding him the last bite on his plate. "You haven't had dessert yet."

"Oh, baby." John leaned back and rubbed his stomach. "Maybe later for dessert. I know I can't eat another bite."

I threw the napkin down on the table, stood up, and grabbed him by the hand. "Good, because this dessert doesn't consist of you eating another bite." I half-smiled and pulled him up out of the chair and led him into the bedroom. My smile faded and I fought back tears the entire way there, but I remained strong.

Once we reached the bedroom, I walked John over to the bed and pushed him down gently by the shoulders, into a sitting position.

"How about a massage, baby?" I untied his robe and slid it off his shoulders.

"Wow! Honey, you're really spoiling me. This is really freaky . . . almost scary." He softly patted me on the behind as I stood in front of him. "Almost like one of those 'Stepford Wives.'" He chuckled. "Is there something I should know? Did you wreck your Jag? Or did you quit your job to pursue exotic dancing? What is it, Angel?" John giggled nervously.

"No, sweetie, it's nothing. A woman can't cater to her man? Speaking of which—" I walked over to the built-in entertainment center and selected disc three in the changer. I then set it to play on repeat Destiny's Child's "Cater 2 U," so I could hear the song over and over.

I turned around and winked.

John licked his lips.

I sashayed over to my dressing table and retrieved a bottle of massage oil that I had ordered from one of those party toy representatives at a bachelorette party I had gone to for one of the girls at the office. I poured some into the palm of my hands and began warming it up by rubbing my hands together. I made my way back over to John.

By the time I reached him, I had activated the warming sensation of the massage oil. I then placed my hands on John's shoulders and rubbed him gently. I smiled to myself as I felt the tension in his shoulders. *So you are a little nervous after all, huh?* I smirked.

He removed his pajama pants, allowing me to rub every part of his body, from top to bottom, and front and back.

Thirty minutes later, he was totally relaxed.

It was time for me to move onto other things. I slowly moved my hands down John's torso, ending at his midsection. He seemed to get hard instantly as I massaged his shaft.

I quickly moved from a hand massage to tongue massage.

John's intense moans were an indication that I had sent him to another world.

Grabbing my head, John guided my motions in tune with the thrust of his pelvis.

My mind began to drift as I thought about his little mistress. I wondered if he grabbed her the same way, if he'd moaned with each stroke, just like he was doing now.

Just as my mind began to fume and I thought about biting his dick instead of sucking it, my mouth filled with the warm, bitter taste of his ejaculation.

Saved by the bell, you bastard!

John had just saved himself from a twisted Hannibal Lector-Lorena Bobbitt performance. I lifted my head slowly, sure to look as pleasing as possible. I sucked every drop of cum from his penis.

John shivered with pleasure as my tongue reached the head of his penis.

I licked off the final drop then tilted my head back and swallowed as though I was taking a shot of Patron.

"Damn, Angel! I don't think you've ever given me head like that before," John said, astonishment in his voice.

It was time for me to execute my plan.

"That's just the beginning, baby. I think we should explore other areas of our sex life."

"What! I thought you were happy with our sex life?" John responded, sounding offended.

"Oh, I am, baby. It's not me; it's you I'm worried about."

"Me? Angel, what's going on? Where is this coming from?"

I could tell John was beginning to get a little worried. Although I enjoyed seeing him balance on one foot on the tight rope of curiosity, I had to stay focused on my plan.

"Well, the ladies and I were having a really interesting conversation today at the spa. Basically, we were discussing how you must please your man in the bed because, what you won't do, there is always another woman willing to do it. So it made me think of areas that maybe I was a little closed-minded on like oral sex, anal sex, and threesomes. So far I've crossed one bridge; now it's time to cross the others." I sat on my knees and spoke in a serious tone. "Let's maximize our sexual experience—What do you say?"

At first, John didn't respond; he just looked at me in disbelief.

"Is this some type of trick, Angel?"

"Sweetie, no. Some of the ladies have experienced all of the things I've mentioned, and they gave me some wonderful tips—the do's and don'ts and what to expect."

Jonathan gave me a look as if to ask, "Are you for real?" He then just shook his head. "I don't know, Angel, all of this has kind of taken me by surprise."

I could tell that he was trying to play it safe. He desperately wanted to explore the sexual areas I had mentioned, but at the same time, he wanted to be sure that I wasn't trying to trick him into admitting that he wanted to be with another woman besides me.

"I won't take no for an answer. I want us to have a threesome, and I'm leaving it up to you to choose the woman," I demanded, leaving no room for him to say no.

"Baby, I don't know anyone; I don't even know how to approach a woman with such a request."

"John, it's really simple. We live in Atlanta, honey. Forty percent of the women here are bisexual. I'm sure there's got to be a woman or two from your job that are hot for you. I'll give you a week. Let me know when you have someone." I pulled the covers back and snuggled up under them. "Now let's go to sleep. It's getting late. I love you." I kissed him. "Oh, and turn that CD off for me, would you?"

Little did he know, that was the kiss of death, the kiss Judas gave prior to the Crucifixion. If things were to go as planned for our threesome, John would choose that little tramp I saw him with earlier, and by doing so, he would be stepping into a deadly love triangle.

CHAPTER 4

Jonathan

"Indecent proposal"

Damn that was some million-dollar head, I thought to myself while massaging my dick. Angel had never given me head like that before. It's like she'd taken some sort of "suck dick right" course—Blowjob 101.

I used to complain about the money she spent at the spa, but that shit finally paid off! I have to admit, it was rather scary that Angel chose the day and time I'd just left Danielle to give me the royal treatment. But oh well . . . good head like that, I'd take it any day it comes.

One thing I can say though, that shit about keeping your man happy ain't nothing but the truth. Hell, that's why I have Danielle on the side now. Angel was always on some old goody-goody shit and wasn't trying to please a man in the bed, but Danielle, she gets wild! Now a nigga is getting the best of both worlds. Shit's starting to seem too good to be true. I had Danielle who was down for whatever, and now suddenly my wife was down for whatever too; the best of both worlds indeed.

As Angel lay next to me, sleeping sound after making me cum and making her demand, I had to pinch myself to see if I was dreaming.

Looks like I'm gonna have my cake and eat it too. Wait until I tell the niggas about this shit. They ain't never gonna believe me.

Every man's fantasy was about to be my reality. The only trick was to get Danielle to agree to a threesome. I figured she would resist in the beginning, but I had a week to work on her. She was the type who liked nice things, but she liked being admired, and to be shown appreciation and admiration. And more than anything, she had to be given time.

That's where that ballplayer fiancé of hers was fucking up. Like most athletes, he was into the parties, his home boys, and the media, and had no time for the wifey, leaving the door wide open for small-time ballers like myself to fuck his girl.

I glanced over at Angel who was dead asleep. I kissed her gently on her cheek, admiring her beautiful face. It was times like these that made me wonder why the hell I even cheated on my wife in the first place. But we all know why—It's because we men think with the smallest head, hoping to get brain, instead of thinking with the head that already has a brain.

I slowly pulled the sheets back and crawled out the bed, sure not to wake Angel. I crept into the living room to give Danielle a call before I went to sleep. Not only did I need to oil her up to pop the big question, but we also needed to discuss my little outburst I had during sex earlier.

As I dialed her phone number, I decided that I may or may not pop the big question; it all would depend on how the conversation flowed.

"Hi, Jonathan," her sweet voice sang as she answered the phone.

"What's up, gorgeous? Sorry for calling so late. I just wanted to call and wish you luck on your case tomorrow." As always, I was playing the caring role.

"Oh, thank you! That's what I love about you, Jonathan—You are so thoughtful."

"This is the big case, right . . . the one at the circuit court? Your chance to prove to the firm you can successfully work a big case?" I let her know I knew all the specifics.

"Yes, it is. Glad to know you are really interested in my career."

It seemed she was impressed that I actually paid a little attention when she talked.

The conversation was going smooth so far. It was just that simple—a few thoughtful words brightened her up. I'd scored a few brownie points; step one to getting her to agree to a threesome with Angel and me.

Now I had to decide if I should be direct and discuss the "I love you" statement from earlier. I didn't want to fuck up my chances of getting both my wife and my mistress in bed though, so I decided to go forth in working my way towards the topic of a threesome.

"You know, my wife and I had the strangest conversation tonight," I casually mentioned.

"Oh really? What did you all talk about?"

"Well, it seems like her day at the spa had a huge impact on her today. Evidently, she and some of the young ladies there had a little 'please-your-man' chat," I said, saying just enough to tease Danielle's curiosity.

" 'Please-your-man chat'?"

"Yeah. She came home catering to me in every way—dinner, massage, sex. Then she talked about how we should maximize every sexual experience."

"Oh really? And just how does she suggest you all do that?" Danielle definitely sounded intrigued at this point.

I used this to my advantage. "Well, as you know from previous conversations, Angel was never really a winner in the bed. Hell, you practically turned me on to every exotic sexual experience there is. Well, now Angel is trying to step up to the plate, even though there isn't much she can offer me at this point because you and I have just about done it all. But when she voiced one suggestion in particular, my mouth nearly dropped to the floor in disbelief," I said, choosing my words carefully.

"Umph. She wants to please her man and step up to the plate now. Well, I guess that leaves little room for a mistress now, doesn't it?" Danielle's tone was bitter.

I figured that was her indirect way of asking if this was my way of trying to dump her. Regardless of her reasoning, that was the perfect response. It was the perfect set-up for my proposition.

"You know, Danielle, you're absolutely right. With Angel's new-found sexual freedom, I guess you could call it, there's little need for a mistress." I tried to intentionally upset her.

"So I guess this is goodbye then, huh?"

"I guess, in a way it is."

"What do you mean, 'in a way,' Jonathan?"

"Well, you see, it will be goodbye, mistress, and hello, mutual sex partner," I hinted.

" 'Mutual sex partner'?—Okay, Jonathan, enough of the games—Just let me know what the deal is."

There was no more beating around the bush. My plan to gain Danielle's interest and tricking her into thinking the worse, had worked. Now it was time to just lay things out flat.

"Okay, Danielle, you asked for it straight, so here it is." I took a deep breath. "Angel wants to have a threesome." I rushed out the words, nearly turning a six-word sentence into a six-syllable word.

"Excuse me? I don't think I heard you correctly—'Angel wants to have a threesome'?"

"Yes, baby, she does. She even wants me to pick the woman. When she asked, you were the only one that came to mind. I know this may seem sort of strange, but think about it—we'll no longer have to hide—What a convenience; things couldn't be better." I was trying my best to convince Danielle that this was an opportunity that not every man and his mistress were fortunate enough to be presented with.

"I don't know, Jonathan. I mean, I've never done anything like this before."

I didn't know how to read her last statement. Was she truly contemplating it, but was a little hesitant because she had never done anything like that before? Or was she acting like one of those girls who tells a guy that she had never sucked dick before, but had worn the skin off her knees and had semen stains on her tonsils?

"Well, it's just an option, baby." I tried to downplay the entire idea. "Like I told you earlier, I love you, Danielle, and I can't think of anyone else I would rather share this experience with. I don't want you to feel forced. Just sleep on it. We'll talk about it more in the morning, if you'd like."

She sighed. "Okay, Jonathan, but I'm not going to lie, this is a bit much to swallow. I will sleep on it, and maybe we can do a late lunch tomorrow and discuss things further. Besides, I owe you a make-up lunch anyway."

We both chuckled.

"Well, I gotta go. Big case in the morning. Good night, Jonathan."

"Good night."

"Yes!" I balled a fist and lifted my knee. I was confident that I had won Danielle over. I knew that she would deliver. I could tell by her responses that she was gonna agree; otherwise she would have already told me no. No matter whether she agreed out of selfishness to show me that Angel could never compare to her, or because she genuinely wanted to do it out of love for me, she was gonna come through.

Although I really didn't get to discuss the issue of me allowing those three little words to slip from my lips while having sex earlier, I was glad to have at least gotten past one hurdle.

I headed back to the bedroom and slid back in bed next to Angel, sure not to wake my lovely wife. Once again, I kissed her beautiful face.

Thank God for beauty shop gossip.

I never thought a sane dude would ever say those words, but any nigga in my shoes would have to give praise to those chatting fools at the spa.

Chapter 5

Ceazia

"Girls gone wild"

"What the fuck was I thinking?" I said to myself while washing my tears away in the beads of water that fell on my face. Parlay's big day had finally come and things had surely gone wrong, wrong, wrong. I couldn't believe the shit that had just gone down tonight. I wasn't ready for that shit at all.

The so-called threesome didn't happen anything like my threesome with Vegas on our Cancún vacation. I know I ain't no *ménage à trois* queen, but I had at least experienced it once. On top of that, I had heard many stories and seen enough pornographic videos to know a little something-something. I knew enough to know that the shit that just went down tonight wasn't how a *ménage à trois* is supposed to go down. It was the furthest thing from a fantasy, something more like a nightmare.

As I stand here letting it replay over and over in my mind again, I still can't believe Parlay would do such a thing. It was like this nigga had just lost his damn mind or something.

Everything was going as planned in the beginning. Dinner was perfect, his party at the strip club was a ball, and when he saw his dessert, he was delighted. But it was at the after-party when he did the ultimate act, that pushed me to the limit. A dessert that had started out as sweet as cotton candy, turned as bitter as malt vinegar.

Our night started off lovely, with a quiet dinner on the deck of Parlay's house. I had hired our own personal chef to come out and cook for us Hibachi style. We sat overlooking the river from Parlay's deck. The night was beautiful and the stars were shinning bright. The bonfire and candles blended perfectly with the shining stars and full moon above us. The atmosphere was so romantic, like something out of a movie when America is being introduced to its next Hollywood sweetheart.

I had hired a pianist and violinist to play. We sat side by side, staring into each other's eyes, taking in the melodies. The musicians were awesome. They started off playing classical, but then they flipped it by playing some of Parlay's rhythm and blues and soul favorites.

"Happy birthday, baby," I said over an instrumental of one of Alicia Key's songs. "I hope you've enjoyed everything I've planned." I massaged my man's perfectly manicured hands.

"Baby, just sitting here with you alone is much more than a nigga could expect. You know most cats can't even appreciate shit like this. Hell, most of these hoodrats out here wouldn't even be able to put some shit like this together for their man."

"I'm glad you're happy. I have to admit, though, at first I had no idea where to begin. Hell, what do you get a guy that has everything?"

"Well, you did a damn good job, shortie. Ain't no chick ever done nothin' like dis for a nigga befo'," Parlay said in country slang.

I had no problem doing whatever it took to secure this nigga. I knew he was my meal ticket. The least I could do was be his appetizer; putting out in order to secure the meal. True, I wasn't even getting much in return, but that's what made things work in my favor. You see, with guys of Parlay's caliber, you have to come at them from a different angle. They expect chicks to be at them for their money and fame. So when a chick comes along and pays for shit, never asks for anything, declines trips, and does thoughtful things, instead of being the ordinary begging bitch, she sticks out from all the others. And right now, I was sticking out like a sore thumb.

Once the chef had delivered us the final course of his meal, a fried ice-cream dish, I tipped him and the musicians, and sent them on their way.

It was time for Parlay and me to head to his favorite strip club, Bottoms Up. I'd reserved the VIP section for Parlay and ten of his boys. Of course, as soon as we arrived he had his choice of any chick in the club to dance on him. But there was this one girl in particular that he'd had his eyes set on.

I could remember times he'd come home after a night at the club and tell me about this chick named Juicy. He would tell me how she was so untouchable, compared to the other dancers and blah, blah, blah. So with that said, I'd made it my personal duty to deliver this tasty meal to my baby on a silver platter.

I scanned the club quickly as we entered. It was as though an alarm had gone off as soon as we pulled up to the valet, like in the movie *The Players Club*. When we hit the door, dancers were already heading toward the empty VIP area.

We followed the bouncers closely as we maneuvered our way through the packed club to the area reserved for us. The waitress met us there almost simultaneously.

"Let me get five bottles of Rose," my baby ordered, "and the sweet honey and white chocolate-flavored Cristal.

"Okay, that will be—"

"Start a tab, sweetie." I whipped out my American Express and handed it to the waitress.

"Okay. Will you need anything else with that?" she asked.

"Yes. I need change for five thousand—all twenties. And send over Juicy, please."

The waitress said, "Juicy doesn't do private—"

"Just tell her it's Parlay's birthday and he is requesting her presence." I interrupted the waitress once more.

I already knew the spiel. I'd heard it over and over from

my man. There was no need for the little waitress to even waste her breath telling me. Juicy was the hottest stripper in Atlanta. Renowned for her all-female parties, and envied by every dancer to hit a stage, she'd been in every uncut video on BET.

Granted, the bitch was hot without a doubt, but I think with such accomplishments, things had gone to her head. Now she was on some superstar shit. Juicy had a bunch of high-class rules and shit, one of them being that she doesn't allow one man to halt the money of several men by doing private dances.

She strolls in the club at whatever time she chooses, hits the stage within an hour of her arrival, and once on stage, if the DJ doesn't have the selection of reggae she requests to dance to, she refuses to dance. And until she gets at least a hundred dollars thrown to her feet on stage, she won't even as much as clap her ass cheeks.

But once the money starts flowing in, after five songs of pure sexual enticement, she leaves—no table dances, no private parties, no questions.

But anyone who knew Ceazia knew that those rules didn't apply to me. I'd been in the game; I'd worn her shoes. So I, for one, knew that money talks. At the end of the day—the middle and beginning too—everybody has a price. And tonight I had stacks to spend; eagerly ready to pay the price. I had no problem whatsoever popping rubber bands for that bitch.

I watched as the waitress went to the back and headed for the dressing room.

Five minutes later, she came out alone. I had already figured that her majesty would refuse my initial request. But even so, I still was not discouraged.

The waitress came over shortly after with our drinks and change.

"So what's the deal?" I asked, prepared for the worse.

"She said she will stop by after she comes off stage."

"All right. Thanks." I handed the waitress twenty dollars for her effort.

I already knew the deal. Juicy wanted to see how we tipped while she was on stage, before she even considered coming over. If that was what she was basing her decision on, the decision was already made.

I smiled at the sight of Parlay and his boys popping the bottles and throwing twenties into the air.

Thirty minutes later, Juicy's entrance was announced.

"And now the moment you all have been waiting for," the DJ yelled over the theme music to *Rocky*.

Out of the dressing room walked Juicy, preceded by two young ladies tossing rose petals on the floor. All eyes were on Juicy as she stepped on stage covered by her white cotton robe; her name embroidered on the back and a picture of her face airbrushed underneath it.

She was just too much; way over the top. This shit was not sexy to me. In my opinion, it was damn near comical, but the niggas were going crazy. And as far as Juicy's pockets were concerned, that's all that mattered.

Once Juicy was positioned on stage with her legs spread and hands on hips, the DJ cut the music off.

"Okay fellas, come wid it! Y'all niggas know the routine," the DJ said into the mic, before blasting that rasta shit.

That was my cue. I quickly grabbed a thousand-dollar stack of twenties and headed to the stage. I stood there looking Juicy eye to eye as I peeled off the twenties as though I was dealing a deck of cards, and tossed them to the stage floor.

That's surely gonna get that ass moving.

"Gotdam, shortie!" the DJ yelled.

I continued to peel off twenties, one by one.

"Now all y'all niggas should be embarrassed up in this bitch, letting a broad outspend y'all's broke asses." He laughed. Then he threw on "We Be Burnin" by Sean Paul.

Juicy's robe dropped and underneath it, I must admit, was the baddest body I had ever seen on any female, without the effects of airbrushing. Her honey-bronze skin was like a custom paint job. Every curve and cut seemed to have been hand-carved by God himself. Round and soft, yet firm, her breasts were like the best two cantaloupes out of the entire bunch in the grocer's. It would be difficult to wean any baby off those. Her long, slicked-back, "I-Dream-of-Jeannie" ponytail slithered around her neck like a snake.

In all honesty, she wasn't the best of dancers. As a matter of fact, she didn't really dance at all. Just watching her sway her hips back and forth was enough for the men.

I dropped a couple more twenties and figured I'd scram and allow the fellas frontrow seat.

Just when I thought enough had been said without words

being spoken, and my mission was accomplished, I turned around and landed right in Parlay's arms.

When he spotted Parlay up at the stage the DJ yelled, "Oh shit! Shut the club down! Niggas step ya game up." The DJ stopped the music to announce. "We got muthafuckin' Parlay in this bitch tonight!"

We both smiled.

I turned around to enjoy the rest of Juicy's performance with my baby. I stood at the stage, my man's arms wrapped around my shoulders.

Once again I started throwing twenty after twenty at Juicy's stilettos. Juicy never left the spot on the stage directly in front of us. And even though we half-paid attention to her because we were too busy with our tongues down each other's throat, I was throwing twenties over my shoulder at her. I knew it was a wrap; the deal had unquestionably been sealed!

After Juicy's set was over, she left the stage and rushed toward the dressing room.

I know this bitch ain't trying to play me, I thought as watched her walk her ass right past us.

There was no way this bitch wasn't coming over to holla at my nigga after all that loot I had just dropped for the bitch to twitch her ass a couple of times. I mean, she could have hopped on the pole or something. I don't care if I had to go in the back and drag that bitch out by her weave ponytail, she was gonna give Parlay a fucking table dance tonight.

About twenty minutes and one shot of Patron later, Juicy

came prancing over fully dressed in a Juicy sweat suit and Juicy contour sidekick alike.

"What's up, sexy?" She stared dead at me. "You wanted to see me?"

I wanted to see her ass—but half-naked. How the hell does she expect to give my man a table dance fully dressed?

"Well, actually, I was requesting your presence for my boyfriend, Parlay. It's his birthday," I told her.

"Oh, it's his birthday." Juicy turned her attention to Parlay and headed in his direction. She sang out, "Birthday bbbbbooooooyyyyy," getting his attention.

The look on his face was priceless. He looked up at Juicy and then over at me.

I smiled and nodded my head, indicating that Juicy's presence was all my doing. Now that I had delivered, although not to my full satisfaction since the bitch was fully dressed, I figured I could at least take a potty break.

I forced my way through the crowd and into the ladies room. After checking myself out in the mirror, I headed back to the table, concentrating on my walk. I wanted to make sure that it wasn't obvious to the world that I was tipsy.

I must admit, I felt like I was the shit. I had single-handedly orchestrated the best birthday I was sure that Parlay had ever experienced in his life. I couldn't wait to get back to the table and watch him continue to enjoy his night.

When I got back to the table, I was surprised at the sight before me. There stood Miss Juicy with her 5'-9" frame, 36C breasts, 26-inch waist, and all forty inches of her ass all out on top of the table, giving Parlay a table dance. The saying couldn't be anymore true—muthafuckin' money talks!

I allowed Parlay to enjoy his gift. I sat off to the side, sipping on a bottle of water. I watched Parlay and his boys wild out. I smiled to see him having such a great time. I patted myself on the back. I was proud for putting together such a wonderful night. But the best part had yet to come.

The skinny, little waitress that had served us the entire night, interrupted my moment of joy.

"Excuse me."

"Yes," I responded, full of attitude.

"The owner would like to speak with you," she stated nervously.

Now what? I knew shit was going a little too smoothly. As soon as I was congratulating myself for such a wonderful night, I have drama. I couldn't imagine what the hell the owner had to say.

" 'The owner'? For what?"

"She didn't say, but if you could follow me—"

"No, ma'am. I cannot follow you anywhere. If the owner would like to speak to me, then she needs to come over here—Can't you see it's my man's birthday? And I've paid good money for the cake."

The waitress walked away without saying another word.

I focused my attention back on Parlay and Juicy, who hadn't even noticed the small confrontation between the waitress and me.

"Excuse me."

I felt a tap on my shoulders.

"Yes," I said, ready to blast whoever it was disturbing me for the second time.

When I turned around, I froze with astonishment; we froze with astonishment. I couldn't believe my eyes, and I was sure she couldn't believe hers either. I didn't know if I should jump on this bitch or hug her. I hadn't talked to her in years, and I didn't know her position. From the look in her eyes, she didn't know if she should hug me or call for security.

"What's up, Chastity?" I said, deciding to break the ice.

"What's up, C? How have you been?"

Unsure of her vibe, I kept it short. "I'm good." I looked her up and down. "So what's up?"

"Oh, well, I was just coming over to thank you all for your business and to offer you all a picture on our wall of fame. I had no idea—"

"Yeah, I know. You had no idea it was me. I'll get Parlay and the fellas together, so you can get your picture. Send the picture man over."

"All right. Will do." Chastity walked away. "Oh and, C"—She stopped and turned around—"uh, I'm glad to see you again."

I shook my head and smiled to myself. *Like hell, you are.* My high was now fully blown. I had no idea what to really think about Miss Chastity.

I walked over to the table where Parlay and the fellas were still enjoying Parlay's personal birthday present.

"Excuse me, baby." I tapped Parlay on the shoulder. "The club owner wants a picture for her wall of fame."

"Cool," Parlay said, not taking his eyes off of Juicy.

I then gave all his boys word too.

Chastity returned with the cameraman at her side. "You all ready?"

Oblivious to everything going on around him, Parlay was steady in agreement. "Let's do it."

All his boys gathered around him.

I made my way to Parlay's side.

We all smiled for the camera as the picture man took a couple of shots. Then they all went right back to partying as before.

Chastity lingered around for a moment. When she thought it was safe to strike up a conversation, she asked, "So what brings you here?"

"Just celebrating my boyfriend's birthday."

"I see." She shook her head.

After a few more seconds of watching Parlay and his friend's celebrate, she said, "Well, I guess I better get back to work. Here's my card. Give me a call some time." She hugged me before leaving.

I wasn't sure what to make of that. Chastity and I were friends from a long time ago, but after Vegas' and Meikel's death, she, along with several other chicks I thought were my friends, all disappeared. I assumed they had all disassociated themselves from me because they figured I was responsible for Meikel's death. This was the first time I'd seen anyone from my old crew since the murders.

I placed Chastity's card in my purse and glanced at the

time. My watch read 1:00 a.m. It was about that time for the fat lady to do her thing.

After a performance of a lifetime, five thousand dollars worth of tips and a matching tab later, the party was finally over. Now it was on to the after-party.

I called Diamond to give her a heads-up that we were on our way. I ran down the blueprint one last time, for my own personal reassurance, to the most memorable sexual experience that either of us would ever engage in. It was simple—Diamond was there as his love slave; nothing more, nothing less. Whatever Parlay wanted, Diamond was to deliver. I didn't care if he wanted to stick his penis in every hole on her body. As his personal love slave, she was to agree.

I considered myself a freak in the bed, but Parlay was definitely on a whole 'nother level. One thing was for sure—Diamond was in for more of a ride than a cowgirl at a rodeo.

When we arrived home, Parlay had no idea that the party was actually just beginning. As we entered the house, Parlay did what he had done the entire way home—thank me for the special evening I had arranged for him.

A huge mischievous grin on my face, I didn't reply. I just took him by the hand and led him to the bedroom. As we made it to the bedroom doorway, I released his hand and allowed him to enter ahead of me.

He drunkenly stumbled into the room.

The bedroom set-up was beautiful. I had, had Diamond sprinkle rose petals all over the floor. There was soft instrumental music, over fifty tea light candles, and, last but not least, Diamond spread across the bed like a duvet.

"What the fuck?" Parlay slurred his words. He stared at Diamond. "Baby, this is just too much. This shit is crazy!"

Parlay was like a kid watching a magic show. He couldn't figure out the trick. He just stood there, dick hard and with a Kool-Aid smile.

It must have been obvious that I was going to need some help snapping him out of his trance, because Diamond got up and led him and me both to the bed by the hand.

Once we reached the bed, she turned around and faced each of us. She looked at me and then kissed me on the lips. She then looked at Parlay and kissed him on the lips. Slowly, Diamond unbuttoned Parlay's button-up and slipped it off his shoulders.

"Raise your arms," she said softly to me. After sliding my shirt over my head, she placed her arms around me and unsnapped my bra as she French-kissed me.

Once the bra met my shirt on the floor, Diamond made her way back over to Parlay and began unbuckling his belt. The next thing I know, his pants dropped to his ankles, and her tongue was now down his throat.

After she undressed each of us, our erotic experience began. Diamond sat down on the bed, and Parlay and myself stood before her, in complete nakedness.

Diamond started with me. She pulled me by the hand down onto the bed.

I found myself sitting next to her. Although I was a bit

nervous at first, I actually began to feel more comfortable as things went on.

"Lay down," she whispered. She pushed me back.

I lay there, my legs hanging off the bed. Diamond kneeled before me and kissed my things. Not long after, her tongue was flicking at my clit. I was amazed at the enjoyment I received from her.

Once Diamond realized how into it I was, my hips thrusting back and forth, she got up abruptly and had me scoot up to the head of the bed. She then laid me back down on my back and placed my legs on her shoulders as she licked me from nipple to clit then back up again.

When she was at eye level with me, she did the trick that surprised me the most. While lying directly on top of me, as though she had a penetration stick of her own, Diamond spread my legs and pressed her vagina directly on top of mine. With pressure she grinded, and before I knew it, my body was sent to ecstasy!

"Aaaahhhhh," I screamed with pleasure. "Diamond," I called out. I couldn't believe a bitch had me calling out her name, but I was feeling too good to be jealous. Diamond had definitely taken me to another level.

Even Parlay was into it. He stood over us, watching, stroking his dick up and down.

"I told you, you wouldn't be disappointed," Diamond whispered between small nibbles on my ear.

And she was right. I was not disappointed; instead I was overly pleased, almost to the point of disbelief. I'd never felt such an amazing feeling without penetration. Only a man could make me feel so good. I lay in silence, flabbergasted, my body gyrating independently with pure delight.

Constantly monitoring Parlay, I could tell he was pleased at the sight before him.

Diamond laid him down between us, and we took turns sucking his penis and his nipples.

Parlay's eyes rolled to the back of his head in pleasure. His erection hard as a rock, he pulled me on top of him so that I was riding him backwards.

Diamond sat in front of me, her legs around my waist, and began sucking my breasts and massaging my clit as I slowly bounced up and down on Parlay's manhood.

"Oh shit," he moaned. He lifted his upper body up off the bed, grabbed me, and pressed me down hard on him.

I knew he was ready to jerk. Not wanting him to reach his peak, I lifted up and handed him a condom, as an indication that it was time for him to sex up Diamond.

After securing the condom on his dick that was so hard and tight that his veins were pulsating, he bent Diamond over and entered her from the back.

Wanting her to work that magic tongue of hers again, I crawled up underneath her and spread my legs wide.

She smiled, and taking the hint, she buried her pretty little head between my legs. Like a snake, her tongue slithered up into my pussy and sent a feeling through me like I'd never felt before, almost shocking me. In and out, her tongue plugged me up like a dick.

I looked up at her in astonishment.

She gave me one of the most seductive looks I'd ever seen. It was then that I knew what she was trying to do. She made it clear she wanted me, and that was exactly what she was trying to do—have me and please me, with the hopes that after our little threesome, I'd continue wanting her. Just her. She wanted to make sure that she would get me so far gone that she could have me.

Shit, I have to admit it did feel good, but not good enough to pull me from dick. Sad to say, but it wasn't happening.

Her mouth covered my clit area, and warmth penetrated my skin that made cum run out of me like a faucet.

Diamond sat up and smiled a smile of victory. I guess she figured she'd accomplished what she had set out to do. She got up on her knees and started throwing her ass back at Parlay.

I lay there trying to recuperate from the sudden explosion in my body. I mean, I was so taken by Diamond that I'd almost forgotten about Parlay. I sat up on my elbows and glanced up at them.

Diamond's eyes were closed, and her hand was between her legs, stuffing Parlay's dick inside of her as he slowly stroked deep inside her.

My heart skipped a beat when I saw him passionately kiss Diamond's neck and whisper in her ear, "Give me that wet pussy, baby. Give me that good, wet pussy." He began stroking her hair and continued to whisper in her ear.

I could feel my eyes turn red as I stared at him. I lay motionless, my blood boiling. Not wanting to ruin the mood, but definitely needing to stop the madness, I gently pulled Diamond towards me.

As she came down on me, Parlay was left on his knees with a hard, wet dick.

I turned Diamond over onto her back and began kissing her passionately.

Parlay grabbed my waist, ready to bang me from the back.

I grabbed his penis to remove the condom, and again my heart nearly dropped out—there was no condom. *Where the fuck was the condom?—I know he didn't remove it during the switch.*

It was hard to continue, but I continued to kiss Diamond while he fucked me from behind. At that point, my vibe totally ruined, I wanted him to just cum and get this over.

"Cum for me, baby! Come in this wet pussy," I begged, hoping to speed along the process.

"No, baby, not yet. Come suck my dick. I want to cum in your mouth," Parlay groaned.

I happily agreed. Hell, anything just to get that shit over with. It wasn't turning out to be the big birthday surprise I had hoped for after all, at least not for me. But anyway, I sucked away as Diamond stood next to Parlay and he began to finger her.

I closed my eyes, hoping that when I opened them, I would wake up and this would all be just a bad dream. But when I opened them, Parlay was tonguing her down like he was a marine who had been out to sea for six months.

My first instinct was to just get up and walk out, but

there was no way I was leaving them alone together. Hell, at the rate they were going, they might've fucked around and made a baby. Instead of ruining things, I just closed my eyes again and prayed for the escapade to be over.

A few more minutes and my throat was splashed with Parlay's warm liquids. I opened my eyes to what I thought would be relief. Instead, it was hell before me—Diamond's pussy covered Parlay's face.

She had stood up and rested her foot on his shoulder while he ate her out. There she sat moaning in ecstasy on his face as he squeezed her ass like he was sucking the juice from an orange.

It took all I had to keep from kicking that bitch in the back of the head and choking the shit out of Parlay. I should have seen it coming, though. It had already been two fuck-ups. I should have never let it get to three.

I got up from the bed right as Diamond began to quiver.

Parlay didn't hesitate to swallow every ounce of her cum.

I wanted to throw up. "Well, I guess the party is over," I said with a fake smile, as an indication it was time for Diamond to get the hell out. I didn't even give her the chance to try to lay down on the bed and recuperate.

She must have gotten the drift, because a few minutes later, she was dressed, and I was escorting her to the door.

"Bye, baby," she said, attempting to give me a goodbye kiss.

"Bye." I quickly stepped aside and closed the door, meaning, *No thanks to the kiss, and get the fuck out*!

CHAPTER 6

Danielle

"In the heat of the night"

Ring, ring, ring, ring, ring!

I woke to the sound of a ringing phone. "Hello?" I answered. Assuming it was Jonathan calling me back, I didn't even look at the caller ID.

"What up, beautiful?" Shawn's raspy voice emerged from the other end of the phone.

Heavily exhaling in frustration, I rubbed my eyes in an attempt to focus at the clock on the nightstand—3:58 a.m. *What the fuck does Shawn want in the middle of the damn night*?

"Yo!" he yelled into the phone again.

"Yes, Shawn." I answered in my most annoyed tone.

"Open the door."

I sat up in my bed and began to look around my room frantically. *Please tell me this is not happening.* I struggled to get out of my bed and put on my robe. I briskly tiptoed to the front door.

"Danielle," Shawn yelled into the phone.

"Yes. I'm still here," I said softly as I walked toward the front door and looked through the peephole. I was relieved to see there was no one in sight—Shawn was just trying to fuck with my head.

"So what's taking so long? Open the damn door, girl," Shawn demanded once again.

"Shawn, shut the fuck up!" I had a lot more courage, now that I saw he was just trying to scare me. "It is four in the morning. I do not have time for your damn games."

I untied my robe as I headed back towards my bedroom.

"What?"

"You heard me, nigga," I said, stopping and stomping my foot and then proceeding to my bedroom.

Spsh! spsh! spsh! Boom!

My journey was interrupted by the sound of gunshots.

I screamed as I fell to the floor in the hallway, dropping the cell phone. I lay on the floor motionless.

I heard steps coming in my direction. Unsure what to do, I grabbed my heart and paced my breathing. That now-much-too-familiar chest pain shot through my body.

"I didn't want to get ignorant, boo-boo, but you made me."

I could hear the voice around me, and through the cell phone in front of me.

That's when I realized exactly who it was. Pissed, but at the same time relieved that I didn't get hit, I slowly lifted myself from the floor.

Shawn stood before me, gun still in hand and smoke rising from the silencer.

I struggled to my feet.

"Why you couldn't just open the door, baby girl?" He asked as though it was my fault he'd just gone postal.

"Shawn, I went to the front door and I didn't see you out there."

Using the same old "dope-boy knowledge" he'd used prior to going to jail, he said, "Come on, Danielle, you should know me better than that. I was at the back door. You actually think I would stand at the front and cause a commotion? All these whiteys around . . . Shit, Bad Boys would be here in no time."

Still a little shaken up, I walked on into my bedroom, and Shawn followed right behind me.

"So what do you want, Shawn?" I was hoping for an easy fix.

"Come on, you know what I want."

I prayed it was his money and not pussy. I'd much rather pay him than screw him. All of a sudden I regretted entering the bedroom in the first place.

"Please, Shawn. It's late. I don't have time for the games. What's up?"

I'd just played twenty-one questions with Jonathan, and surely wasn't in the mood for another round. Only this time, it would be dope-boy knowledge.

"Well, it's a couple of things." Shawn rubbed his hands together and paced back and forth. "For starters, you can come off my cash. Now I ain't no crazy nigga, so I know you done dug into it a little. So I'm gonna give you a break—all I need is one hundred fifty grand; we'll write off the rest—

I'll charge that spending to the game." Shawn looked at me for approval.

Shawn wasn't a dumb nigga by far, but he had to be stupid to think I still had one hundred fifty thousand dollars for him. Hell, it was more like fifty grand, but I refused to tell him that, especially with that gun still in his hand.

"Okay, Shawn, I'll give you your money." I sighed. I folded my arms and flopped down on the edge of the bed. "And once I do that, will you leave me alone?"

"Maybe." He responded with a smirk across his face.

And just what the fuck is that stupid-ass grin across your face for? I stared at him for a moment and then rolled my eyes. "Whatever. Shawn, I'm getting married soon, and I'm up next for partner with one of the best law firms in Atlanta— This is too much to lose from fooling around with some convicted felon. So I beg you, please leave me alone. Give me a week, and you will have your money. After that, I beg you *Dis-Ap-pear*!"

"What?" Shawn yelled at the top of his lungs, causing me to nearly jump out of my skin.

My mind flashed back to one of the many beatings I'd received from him in the past.

"Nothing, Shawn. I'm just really tired and kind of frustrated. The thought of me losing everything I'd worked so hard for just crossed my mind. I'm sorry. I will give you your money, I promise. But please, Shawn, please don't mess things up for me."

Shawn's phone began to ring. He answered on the first ring. "Hello?" he said.

I heard a deep Jamaican voice on the other end. "Yo! Wha ya deal wit?" He was loud and sounded excited.

"I got you, man. I'm handling some business right now. Give me a week." Shawn walked out the bedroom and out into the hallway.

I sat on the bed as Shawn talked, trying my best to eavesdrop. Unfortunately, I couldn't hear a word he was saying as he walked farther away and into the kitchen. Just as I was getting up to move a little closer to the door, I heard Shawn coming back down the hall.

"A'ight, ma," he said as he entered the bedroom. "One week."

"Yes, one week," I confirmed.

He paused for a minute. "All right then. One week. I'll holla at you in a few days." He headed back towards the back door he'd shot through earlier, which was now hanging from the hinges.

"I'll deduct the money for my door from your money that I owe you," I shouted as he walked away. "Thank you, Lord." I looked up at the ceiling. I then took a deep breath, got up from the bed, and went to the back door.

I examined the size ten Timberland boot print on my door that was a perfect imprint from the black, leather Timberland boots Shawn had been wearing. As if shooting the door off the hinges wasn't enough, this fool went as far as to kick it in too! Luckily I had a fenced-in backyard and a storm door I can lock until I get the back door repaired.

I shook my head as I thought of the destruction that

Shawn's pitiful ass had created. I locked the storm door and headed back to bed.

Once in my room, I prepared to get at least a couple hours of sleep before my day began. I lay down and glanced at the clock one last time—5:00 a.m. I snuggled my pillow and pulled the cover over my head, reflecting back on the events of the night.

And a hell of a night it was.

Jonathan and his wife both had flipped their wings. Earlier, Jonathan came at me from way left field and yelled out that he loved me during sex, and now he's asked me to participate in a ménage à trois with him and his wife.

And Shawn, the crazed dope boy, had some way gotten out of jail and tracked me down. For him to go to the extent of tracking me down and coming all the way to Atlanta from Virginia, only meant that something really had to be up.

I wondered what he had going on. Just what was that phone call about anyway? I was almost positive it had something to do with drugs. Hell, Shawn knew nothing more about life than the drug game. I guess, it's like they say, once in the game, always in the game. And that's exactly why he was gonna have to charge this money loss to the game . . . because I had no intentions of giving him one dime back!

CHAPTER 7

Angel

"Unfulfilled destiny"

"What a wonderful day today it will be." I reached over and turned off the beeping alarm clock and then kissed my cheating, sleeping husband on the lips.

He yawned and stretched. "Oh, are we still on the 'cater-to-your-man' tip?" He rubbed his morning hard-on.

No, we are not, dumb ass. I gave him a pleasant smile. I got up out of the bed and headed to the bathroom to shower. I turned on the water and removed my pajamas as I zoned off into thoughts about the events before me.

Jonathan had no idea I was up listening to his dumb ass on the phone last night. He and his little mistress are both falling right into my trap. This is almost too easy.

I showered quickly and threw on some clothes.

"What's on the agenda today, honey?" John asked as I stood in front of the bedroom mirror, brushing my hair into a ponytail.

Boy, if he only knew—trickery, fuckery, and mystery. "Just heading to the gym right now. I'm not sure about later. We'll see what the day brings."

"Wow! That's the luxury of owning your own business, huh? Maybe I should quit my job so I could be more like you." He laughed.

Then what excuse would you use when you're out cheating? I could only think the remarks I wanted so badly to shout out at him. I grabbed John's keys as I gathered my things.

"Honey, I'm going to drive your car today. Could you get my car detailed for me? It's a mess," I lied.

The truth was that I needed John's keys so that I could make a copy of that key that goes to his little secret love palace.

"Sure, baby, no problem." He kissed me on the forehead and then headed towards the bathroom. "Drive safely," he called before closing the bathroom door behind him.

I grabbed his key and jumped in his car and headed to the store. I made it my first priority to get a copy of the key. There were a couple of keys I wasn't sure what they went to, so I made copies of them. One was certainly the right one.

Once that was done, I called John to see exactly where he was. He'd mentioned he had a meeting this morning and I heard from his conversation with Danielle that she had a huge case this morning, so the both of them should be occupied handling separate matters, leaving their secret love cave open for inspection. But one could never be too sure.

"Hello?" John answered the phone.

"Hey, honey," I said. "Just calling to make sure you were

up and getting dressed. I don't want you to be late for your big meeting this morning," I lied.

"Thanks, sweetie. I'll be heading out the door in about another thirty minutes."

"Yes," I lipped under my breath. I still had a few minutes to check out the place. "Okay, have a good day."

"Thanks, sweetie," he said before going to hang up the phone.

"Jonathan," I called out quickly, hoping to catch him before he hung up the phone.

"Yeah," he said, with a hint of concern.

"I love you," I said softly.

"I love you too. Bye."

The phone clicked in my ear and with that said, I put the pedal to the metal and sped across town to his bat cave.

Once I arrived, I parked a few spots from the condo to avoid chat from any nosy neighbors that may be in the area. I pulled the couple of keys I had copied and discreetly placed one into the door. I knew this was going to be a great day when the door opened on the first try.

I rushed right in. I did a quick take of the house. It was simple, but exquisite. As I observed the simple painting of an orchid in a vase with custom mat and framing, and the porcelain trinkets in the curio, I wondered if this was actually John's place or Danielle's. The place was nicely decorated, almost too nice for a man. Granted, John had plenty of style, but the detail and accessories had the hallmarks of a woman's touch all over it.

"Umph! Furniture purchased from BY DESIGN." I ran

my hand down the soft plush couch with throw pillows. There was a matching chair across from it, separated by the octagon-shaped, glass aquarium table. "I guess this bitch and I have a little more in common besides dick." I continued examining the living room and then moved on to the bedroom, which was just as nicely decorated.

My stomach turned as I looked at the crumbled lavender sheets, fresh from the lovemaking my husband and his whore had made the day before. I thought I was gonna be sick. I ran to the bathroom and hugged the pedestal sink. I took deep breaths, hoping to make the nausea go away. Once I gathered myself, I sat on the toilet to take a few last breaths before leaving the condo—I had seen enough.

As I stood up, I noticed the garbage can to my left, sitting next to the commode. Curious to see if John had used protection with Danielle, I rummaged through it. To my dismay, there was no condom. John didn't even have the decency to protect me from any number of the diseases that tramp could be towing around.

I could no longer hold it, my eyes swelled with tears. I struggled to get out the house as fast as I could. As I made my way out of the bathroom and back through the bedroom so that I could get the hell out of there, I noticed a small object glistening from the corner. I headed over to get a closer look.

I bent down and picked it up off the floor and checked it out. "A diamond earring," I said. "And two carats at that."

Well, one thing was for sure—it didn't belong to John. I

tossed the earring in my purse and headed out the door. Now it was on to my next stop—Atlantic Station.

I drove to the loft apartments I had followed Danielle to yesterday. I pulled into the parking garage and walked to the lobby area. I looked around for any piece of information that would lead to Danielle's apartment number, but there were no clues.

Figuring this portion of the operation hopeless, I headed back to my car. As I returned to my car, a guy in a black Bentley coupe pulled up behind me.

"Yo," he shouted from his car window.

I looked over each of my shoulders. I responded in an annoyed tone to let him know that I wasn't pleased with the method he used to get my attention. "Are you talking to me?"

"Yeah. You parked in my spot, shortie."

I checked out his ride and the jewelry he was bound to catch a cold from. It was just far too much ice. Between his useless obsession with bling and his ghetto lingo, I could already tell that he had to be one of those rappers.

I kept it short in hopes of causing little commotion. "Oh, I'm sorry. I had no idea. I'm leaving now anyway." I pulled out my keys and went to put my hand on the door handle to open it up.

"A few seconds longer and your shit would have been fucked up," he yelled in a joking manner.

"And that would have been a charge—destruction of property." I placed my key in the door.

"One thing about that, shortie, my fiancée is an attorney for one of the biggest law firms in the *A*. She got shit on lock. I could probably go and commit a murder and get away with it, baby doll. Danielle would have me out and find a way to lock *you* up."

His bragging was music to my ears. He could only be talking about the one and only Danielle, my little home-wrecking friend. *How fucking convenient*! Shit was starting to look up for sure.

"Well, good for you," I tried to say in an honest and not sarcastic tone. "I noticed you said *fiancée*"—I began digging in my purse. "Well, let me give you my card. My name is Angel Powell, and I'm a wedding planner." I approached his car.

I didn't notice how fine this man was until I got closer. *Damn! I would trade John's tired ass for this man any day! What the hell is wrong with that bitch? What the fuck would possess Danielle to cheat on this man*?

"Okay, Angel, that's a bet." The young man took the business card I extended to him and placed it in his pocket.

"Not to be rude, but just how far do you think that card will get in that pocket? You'll forget about it, and it will end up at the dry cleaners." I pulled out another card. "Why don't you try putting this one in your wallet?"

"Wow! Feisty lil' thang." He pulled out his Louis Vuitton wallet and placed the card inside.

"I look forward to hearing from you." I headed back towards my car. Just then, I stopped and turned back towards him. "Oh, what is your name?"

"I'm sorry. We didn't properly meet." He placed his car in park and stepped out. "Let's try this again. How you doing? My name is Richard Anderson."

This man towered over my five-foot frame.

I looked up and grabbed his hand. "Nice to meet you, Richard." I shook his hand and hoped that he couldn't see how mesmerized I was by his features.

He gave me the most amazing smile as he looked down at me. "I'll be giving you a call, shortie—and I do mean short." He laughed.

"Looking forward to that, Richard."

I headed back to my car and threw it in reverse. Richard backed up, allowing me to pull out.

I put the car in drive and pulled off. I watched as he whipped his car into the parking spot I had just occupied. The Houston Rockets license plate read LOYAL 1. I wondered just how loyal he truly was as I pulled out of the garage.

Karma, karma, karma . . . that shit is so real! I thought as I headed to the city's Circuit Court, where Danielle's case was being heard, something else I'd overheard Jonathan mention during his phone conversation with her.

What are the chances of me bumping into her fiancé like that? I've really got this bitch in the palm of my hands now. There are so many ways I could take things at this point. Maybe I could do her the same way as she has been doing me, and screw her man. And believe me, I would love to do that. Or maybe I could just spill the beans. But that's too simple, and why would he believe me anyway? It would be too easy for her to get out of that one without solid proof. I definitely have some sorting to do.

I arrived at the courthouse in no time. I parked in the courthouse garage and headed to the court lobby. There I read the docket, located Danielle's courtroom, slid past security who was directing someone to the proper courtroom they should be in, and sat down in the back of the courtroom.

I did all of this in five minutes flat. This was just too easy. Hell, I was only a firearm away from doing a "Brian Nichols."

I sat in the courtroom unnoticed. I scanned each bench so that I was fully aware of my surroundings. I didn't even get to the third bench before I saw John's stupid ass. *Supporting his woman, I see.* Any closer and I would have mistaken him for the defendant in the trial.

I shook my head in disbelief and continued to scope out the area. That was enough for me—I had to leave the courtroom. If John saw me, all of my hard efforts to execute my plan would be in vain.

I quietly tiptoed back out of the courtroom and headed toward the elevators. I wasn't more than ten feet away from the elevators, when I heard the courtroom door open. I looked over my shoulder and saw John step out. He was saying something to the guard and wasn't looking in my direction.

I immediately turned back around and made a beeline to

the stairwell. All the way up on the ninth floor, and trying to avoid contact at all cost, I made a quick detour down the steps. *That was a close call.* I couldn't risk him seeing me. That would have been a little too freaky.

I headed out the courthouse and to my car, glad that I wasn't busted after two close calls in one day.

I entered the garage and noticed a young man comfortably leaning against my car. I could only wonder what this was about. It was only 11 o'clock in the morning, and I had already had enough drama for an entire day.

"Is there a reason why you are leaning against my car like you make the payment each month?"

"Damn, you gotta lot of heart for such a lil' woman," the man said in a deep New York accent.

I had little patience for any bullshit. "Can I help you with something, or should I just scream for help? I mean we are at the courthouse; the place is swarming with police."

"No need for that, ma. I'm here to help you."

"Help me? I doubt there is anything you can do to help me, sweetie. Now if you will excuse me, I would like to get in my car." I softly shoved the young man, attempting to grab the door handle of my car.

"I know you're following Danielle because she is sleeping with your husband." He began to walk away.

Of course, those words caught my attention. The only question is, how the hell did he know all that?

I opened my car door and got into the driver's seat, trying to seem uninterested. I put the car in reverse and backed out. I grabbed the parking ticket from my armrest and headed toward the parking attendant, passing the young man on the way.

I watched his every move as I waited in the line to pay and exit. The longer I waited, the more his words pierced my brain, the more curious I got. *Just who the fuck is he? And how does he know all of my business?*

No longer able to bear it, I put my car in reverse and drove back to the area where he stood.

"I knew you would come back."

"Okay, what's up?—How the hell do you know this stuff?" I asked as if he had only a few seconds to tell me and then I was heading off.

"Baby girl, I'm from the streets. I've been following you just as long as you've been following Danielle. Looks like we're out to grab the same fish," the young man said.

"Oh yeah? And why are you after Danielle?" I was curious to know just how much shit this little bitch had gotten herself into.

"It's a long story, ma—Let's just say, she has something that belongs to me. So if you're willing to work with me, we can do the damn thing together."

"I need to know exactly what's going on between you all before I commit to such a thing. I mean, I'm not trying to go to jail or anything."

"Nah, boo, it's not even on that level. I'll never do any harm to her. She's my ex-girlfriend. I'm just trying to put a lil' heat to her to make her come off the goods, that's all."

It looked like our plans were similar. If this guy knew this much, who knows how much other stuff he knew? I figured it could be to my benefit to collaborate with him, so I agreed.

"Okay. We can put our heads together. You scratch my back, and I'll scratch yours." I looked him up and down. "So what's your name?"

"Shawn. And yours?"

"Angel." I dug out a business card. "Give me a call later. Maybe we can meet some place and talk about things." I handed him the card and then drove off.

This was truly a crazy day. *Karma is a mother*! Things couldn't have been easier. Everything was laid in my lap like it was owed to me; each hour bringing me a step closer to tearing down Danielle's little empire. The ball was definitely in my court, and her man was my most valuable player.

Hope you got game, bitch!

CHAPTER 8

Danielle

“Three’s company”

I was surprised to look across the courtroom and see all three of my men. Believe it or not, I wasn't the least bit nervous about all of them being there. If anything, I was excited by the level of support being shown to me.

Jonathan sat back dressed in an Armani suit as though he was a prosecuting attorney.

Not too far from him sat my husband-to-be, Richard. I was most excited about his presence. Something like this was huge for him. Hell, he was hardly ever in town, and when he was, he was always so busy that I only got a small portion of his time. So for him to take time out of his schedule to come see me do my thing at trial, was just more than amazing to me.

I looked over at him from across the courtroom and blew him a small, indiscrete kiss.

He gave me a tease of that amazing smile of his, and a wink of the eye. *God, I love that man!* My lace Vicki's instantly became soaked. I swear, all Richard had to do was show those pearly whites that complemented his dimples, and he could have any woman he wanted. It was like his smile placed some sort of love spell on every woman that saw it.

All I can say was, "Thank God, he's mine!"

Last, but not least, right in front sat Dario. He hadn't actually gained the title of my man, but until my position of partner was secure, he could title himself whatever he wanted.

I'd worked long and hard to prove myself at the firm, and screwed just as long, to make sure my work didn't go unnoticed. So if the firm didn't see me as the chosen one for partner, then I didn't know who they possibly could.

The bailiff began to announce the judge's arrival. "All rise. The honorable—"

I took a deep breath as I reviewed my notes for the case. This was a done deal. There was no way I could lose the case, but I always liked to be extra prepared. I continued to breathe deeply, but it seemed as though the more I breathed, the more my heart began to pound.

All of a sudden my breathing began to race. I looked around hoping no one would notice. I looked to my left then looked to my right. Beads of sweat began to form on my head.

I could hear the judge say, "Defense, your opening statement," but I couldn't move.

"Ms. Stevens, your opening statement, please," he repeated.

I struggled to my feet. My chest balled up with pain.

Everything around me began to spin. Within seconds everything was black.

"Oh my goodness!" I heard a voice shout. "Someone, get help!"

"Stand back and give her some air."

"Danielle, baby, it's me. Open your eyes, sweetie," a familiar voice said.

I opened my eyes slowly and focused in on the owner of the voice. "Richard?" I attempted to get up.

"Yes, baby. Don't move. We're gonna get you some help."

"What happened?" I touched the huge lump on my head.

"You passed out, honey. Everything is okay though. Just relax."

All I could think about is how I'd ruined everything. What the hell had just happened? This was my big case and I couldn't even get past the opening statement. I could only imagine what the firm partners were thinking.

I was able to get steady on my feet and picked my file up.

"Don't even think about it." Richard took the file out of my hands and put it down on the table.

"I have to, Richard. They're counting on me. I have to prove myself. I can do this, Richard. I'm just a little exhausted is all. I'll be fine."

The paramedics arrived and sat me down and proceeded to check my vitals.

"I'm fine," I assured the male paramedic as he checked my pulse.

He studied my pulse count. "Everything seems normal," he mumbled to his co-worker.

"That's because everything is normal. I'm just fine. Like I was telling my fiancé right here"—I pointed to Richard—"I just overexerted myself these past couple days is all. I'll be all right; trust me, I know my body."

Eventually, the paramedics gave me a clean bill of health for the time being, but instructed me to go see my family doctor. My battle was in vain as with all the excitement and distraction, the judge decided to continue the case until the next morning.

With my head down I packed away my files. I didn't look up because I didn't want to see the look on the prosecution's face. I'm sure they felt as though they had me so nervous with this one that I fainted.

Damn it! I thought to myself. I felt defeated before the game even started.

I stuck my file down into my briefcase and walked away. I didn't say much to anyone. I embarrassingly walked from the courtroom into Richard's arms. He then led me to the parking garage.

We were all the way to his car by the time I realized that we weren't anywhere near the parking level or side of the garage where I had parked.

"My car?" I rubbed my head.

"I'll drive. Baby, we should leave your car here. I don't want you driving home. We can come back up here and pick it up tomorrow."

Although I didn't feel like driving, I really needed some

time alone. My cell phone had been vibrating off the hook, and I needed to talk to Dario to make sure things at the firm were still in my favor.

"It's okay, sweetie. I feel fine to drive. Just follow behind me."

"You sure?" He rubbed my face.

"I'm fine. I promise."

"All right then."

Richard agreed and drove me to my car.

"If you start feeling funny again, just pull over immediately."

"I will." I kissed him on the cheek and then hopped out of the car and got into my own.

I pulled out my cell phone and looked down at it. I had five voice messages and seven missed calls. I returned the calls first.

Dario being the most detrimental, I began with him.

"Danielle, are you okay, sweetie?" he asked first thing as soon as he picked up the phone.

"Yeah, I'm fine. I think it was just my nerves. But forget all of that—what are the partners saying?"

"Oh, don't worry about that. I've made sure all of that is just fine. Of course they were a little worried that you wouldn't be able to continue and defend the case, but I assured them that you are a soldier and that you can handle it. Just don't let it happen twice. You've gotta come in strong; otherwise they are gonna say you aren't well enough to work the case. And we both know you really need this one!"

"I'm so lucky to have you on my side," I said with a sigh of relief. "What would I do without you?" I was really appreciative Dario had my back.

"No—what would I do without *you*? You know, Danielle, when you passed out, something hit me. At that moment, I realized that this is more than just sex between me and you. I mean, I'm really feeling you. It scared me to death, thinking that I might lose you. I thought about the things you go through with Richard, and I know I could treat you better—"

"Dario, please. I can't have this conversation right now." As the impact of his words pierced my brain, my chest began to throb once again.

I knew exactly where the conversation was headed, and I was not trying to go there, definitely not now. And, quiet as it's kept, not even later. I promised Dario we would continue our discussion tomorrow over lunch, and I ended the call.

Next, I called Jonathan. "Hey, Jonathan."

"Well hello there." Jonathan's sweet voice gave automatic soothing. "You had me a little worried. I had to catch myself from running to the front of the courtroom when you collapsed."

"I'm sorry. I've been having those episodes a lot lately, but it's never been that bad."

"Baby, you really should get that checked out. It sounds like anxiety or panic attacks."

"I keep telling everybody that I really am okay, but for you, sweetie, I will call my doctor as soon as I get home."

"You do that, honey. And I'll check up on you later. Take care," he said and then disconnected the call.

And just in the nick of time too.

I pulled into the garage of Richard's loft apartment and whipped into the reserved parking spot.

Richard pulled in right behind me and rushed to the car to help me out.

I must say that I loved the attention Richard was showing me. Had I known this was all I had to do to get a little attention from him, I'da fallen out flat on my face months ago. So the next time I get a little lonely, I'll just pretend to be sick—It's a sad, cruel trick, but it's worth it.

"Let me help you," Richard said as I stepped out of the car."

Although I was perfectly capable of walking alone, I let Richard help me every inch of the way. I relished in the comfort and security of his arms. He didn't know it, but he was leading the blind, as I closed my eyes and trusted him to lead me to where I needed to be, safe and sound.

Once we were in the apartment, he lay me on the bed and brought me some water and the cordless phone to call the doctor.

"I think you should call your doctor, baby. Maybe you're pregnant," he said full of hope.

"Richard!" I said as if he was being foolish.

I knew he wasn't going to let up, so I had him retrieve the phone book for me so that I could look up my doctor's phone number.

I called right away, but not because I thought I might be

pregnant, because that was a very slim chance. I called right away because I had to admit to myself that I was a tad bit worried about my condition.

When the doctor came on the phone, I explained to him everything that happened. He asked several additional questions as well. And sure enough, just as Jonathan had speculated, I was having panic attacks. He suggested I make an appointment with the psychologist and come in for an evaluation. I wasn't too fond of the thought of seeing a head doctor, but if not going to check things out would put my position as partner at risk, I was unquestionably going.

"I'll see you then, Doctor Obetz," I said after confirming the time and date of my appointment.

"So what did the doctor say, Danielle?" Richard eagerly asked as soon as I hung up the phone.

I hated to tell him, but I had to. "Honey, I'm not pregnant. The doctor believes that I'm having panic attacks."

Richard's face saddened.

We'd been having the ongoing issue about my getting pregnant. He wanted a baby so bad and I hadn't been able to give him one. We'd tried everything except for fertilization pills and in vitro fertilization. Of course Richard suggested we pay for the ten-thousand-dollar in vitro procedure a long time ago. But the doctors have told us we are perfectly capable of conceiving naturally, so I would have it no other way.

Besides, deep inside, I didn't want a child right now. I'd

much rather focus on my career, but I could never tell Richard that. Once we were married and half of all his assets belonged to me, sure we can work on having a baby, but until then, no way! The warmth and security his arms provided just wasn't enough. Nothing says *security* to a woman from a man, like a boatload of dead prez.

"Panic attacks?" Richard had a puzzled look on his face. "So what's causing them? Do you think this is having an effect on you not getting pregnant?"

"Richard, honey, listen to me—Panic attacks are a result of stress; it has no direct affect on pregnancy. So please, no more questions right now," I said, obviously frustrated.

"I'm sorry, sweetie. Just relax." He fluffed my pillow and began to undress me.

I could already predict what was going to happen next. Richard began to massage my body. I must admit, although I knew what was in store for me, that massage was really relaxing. It was as though Richard was rubbing all my stress away.

My eyes slowly shut as my body felt totally relaxed.

When Richard finished, I felt his hands lift from my body and his lips replace each spot his hands had previously touched. I was so relaxed that I'd almost forgotten that this was the preliminary to sex.

You see, Richard thought he was so smart. He knew it would be rude and very inconsiderate for him to just come out and ask for sex at a time like this, but there was no way he was going to let the day pass without having sex with me. Knowing him, he's marked his calendar and followed my menstrual cycle, so he knows I'm ovulating. Which means what?—That's right—my chance of getting pregnant is at its greatest.

I didn't bother putting up a fight. Either way, Richard would still come out on top.

CHAPTER 9

Richard

"Bun in the oven"

If I didn't learn anything else from Danielle, I learned to shamelessly ask for, and expect, what I wanted. I know—what could a guy who has everything possibly want? What else, but a replica of himself? No, I don't mean some life-like statue or anything. I wasn't that vain. I mean a mini me. A baby. A Richard Junior. Of course my request came out of left field, so Danielle wasn't too quick to say yes. It took some begging, but she finally came around.

I never broke a sweat. Look at the scenario—if you're Danielle Stevens, and the man that's asking you to be the mother of his child is Richard Anderson, you give him a baby.

Unfortunately, getting her pregnant wasn't as easy as momma explained it. We'd tried everything from basil to ovulation kits, and Danielle still hadn't gotten pregnant. At times I thought she really didn't want to have a baby and that she was probably still sneaking and taking the pill or something. But I couldn't understand why.

Hell, she was dating just about the most eligible bachelor in the NBA. There were women who would've loved to trick a nigga into bearing his seed. So I admit, Danielle had me somewhat baffled.

"Richard," I heard Danielle scream my name from the bedroom as I stepped out of the shower.

"What's up, baby?" I wrapped a towel around my waist and entered the bedroom, where Danielle was standing in the middle of the floor holding my jeans in one hand and a business card in her other.

She threw the jeans down and walked over to me. "What are you doing with this card?" She shoved a card in my face.

Confused by her anger, I tried explaining. "Babe, if you read the card, you will see that she is a wedding planner. I thought you would be thrilled to know that I'm actually taking some initiative to get things rolling with the wedding."

Danielle looked down at the card again. "Oh." She sighed. Not to drown in the puddle of embarrassment she was standing in, she quickly regained her composure. "Well, it's just not like you to have some chick's card in your pocket. I guess I'm just overreacting."

I took the card from her hands and laid it on the dresser. "Why are you up snooping around anyway? Danielle, you need to lie down and get some rest. Quit stressing yourself out; that can't help us with you trying to get pregnant."

"I'd love to get some rest, believe you me." Danielle gave me an apologetic kiss on the lips. "I have to go to the office for a little while."

"What?" I said, removing the towel from around my waist and drying off with it. "Is that all you think about?" I didn't mean to yell, but I couldn't hold back the frustration. She was always in such a rush to go back to work.

"No. Of course work is not all I think about. But making partner is the most important thing in my life right now."

"Danielle, are you serious?" I walked over to my dresser, opened a drawer, and pulled out a pair of pajama pants. "Your job is the most important thing in your life right now? Your fucking job?"

I slipped on my pants and then walked over and sat down on the bed.

"You know what? I wasn't trying to go there, but because this job is so important to you, you don't want to have a baby. You're afraid a baby will ruin your little law career. Just admit it, Danielle—be a woman about your shit."

" 'My little law career.' " Danielle walked over to me. "Maybe to a conceited, most eligible NBA star my career is mediocre, but it's mine and I am not jeopardizing it for anyone. Not even you!"

"Thanks for confirming things, Danielle." I threw my hands up. I got up and went and pulled the covers down on the bed. "Go make partner, since that's most important. Just remember, if you don't take care of home, someone else will." I got in bed, pulled the covers over me and turned my back to her.

"Fuck you, Richard." Danielle stormed out of the room and slammed the door behind her.

What the fuck did I just do? I sat up in bed and contemplated going after her. My comments hadn't helped out the baby situation any, but I meant every word that I had said.

Frustrated, I got out of bed and headed to the kitchen to get something to drink. I grabbed a bottle of water from the fridge and then headed back to my bedroom.

As I passed the dresser, I stopped and picked up Angel's card. I took a sip of my water and then contemplated for a moment. I decided to give her a call. I figured Danielle would be impressed if I was able to show her some wedding invitations or location ideas or colors, or something. That should be enough to make up for our little argument, with certainty that some make-up sex will follow. *That will probably be the one time she does get pregnant.*

I got the phone, sat down on the bed and dialed the phone number on the business card.

"This is Angel," a female voice sang from the other end of the phone.

"Hey, Angel. This is Richard."

"Oh, yes. Hello, Richard."

I could tell she remembered exactly who I was.

"I didn't expect to hear from you so soon."

"I didn't expect to call so soon, but I figured I'd surprise the wifey and get things rolling a bit."

"Okay. Well, when and where would you like to meet to discuss things?"

"How about the Atlanta Fish House." I had been having a taste for seafood.

"Perfect. Let's say tomorrow at noon," she suggested.

"See you then." I quickly agreed.

When I pulled up to the restaurant, I got out and handed my keys to the valet. As I headed towards the doors, I saw Angel standing there waiting for me.

She looked down at her watch. "On time. Impressive."

"I handle my business." I held the door open for her entrance.

We were seated right away.

After ordering our drinks and appetizers, Angel immediately jumped right into business. "So let's start with the basics."

I couldn't help but to get a bit distracted by the sight of her perfect breasts that seemed to just jump out at me. In between her comments, I nodded, forcing my eyes to stay focused on her face.

"Richard . . ."

My fantasy was interrupted by Angels call—"I'm sorry, what did you say?" I shook my head back to the business at hand.

"What colors is your wife interested in?"

Honestly, I had no idea, and on top of that, I really didn't care. I was just trying to score a few make-up points to get past Danielle's and my little disagreement. There was no sense in faking the funk, so I just came out and told Angel the real.

"Look, Angel, I'm gonna be honest with you—I have no idea what my fiancée wants. I was hoping to get things started to impress her. I fucked up with her last night, so I'm trying to win her heart back."

"Aw, how sweet," she said, sipping her tea that the waitress had brought to the table. "Okay, let me help you out here. I'm going to start by asking you a few questions so that I can get a feel of her personality, and we can go from there."

Angel asked a hundred and one questions, from Danielle's work to her leisure. By the time she finished with all those questions, I thought she should be able to plan the entire damn wedding with no assistance from Danielle or me.

An entrée and dessert later, Angle's and my discussion was done. With the one piece of information I was able to provide—the actual wedding date—Angel was able to give me plenty of starting points.

She had already chosen a few possible locations to include indoors and outdoors, from churches to ballrooms. She had also brought some color swatches and samples of invitations. I must say, the girl knew her stuff. I was impressed.

"Thank you so much. I'm sure my wife would be pleased," I said as I paid the bill.

"You know what would be even more pleasing?" She grabbed her purse and stood up.

I threw the tip on the table and followed suit. "What is that?" I was open to anything that could make my situation even better.

"It would be great if you planned the entire wedding alone. I mean it's not every day that I go over color swatches with the groom-to-be," she said as we headed towards the exit. "I think your effort is to be commended. Usually it's the bride-to-be who always has the stress of wedding planning. Why don't you take on that responsibility? I mean, it will be a first, but I'll walk with you each step of the way."

I thought about it for a moment as we headed out of the restaurant door and waited for the valet to bring us our cars. Angel's arrived first, and I still hadn't given her a definite yes. That was a hell of a task and I expressed my concerns to Angel, but she assured me we could do it. With her experience, she made it seem as though she could plan a wedding on a day's notice. So how hard could me picking out a few color swatches be?

Needless to say, I agreed. How could I refuse such an offer? This was sure to get me back into the good graces of Danielle.

"Share the information I've given you and show her the samples as well. Give me a call tomorrow and we'll move on to the next step." Angel jumped into her Jaguar.

"Bet, I yelled back." I walked over to my Range Rover the valet driver had just pulled up. After handing the driver a tip, I hopped in and drove off.

Things went pretty well. I can't wait to share this with Danielle.

I headed to RUN AND SHOOT to ball with the fellas. Once I pulled into the parking lot, I grabbed my gym bag from the backseat and dialed up Danielle. The phone rang continuously, but she didn't answer.

I left her a message informing her that I had a surprise for her. "If this doesn't get me a baby, I don't know what will." I threw my gym bag across my shoulder.

CHAPTER 10

Ceazia

"Give them an inch . . ."

"Ungrateful little fucker." I mumbled to myself as I straightened the small mess left from my ecstasy nightmare last night. I was vexed to hear Parlay tell me that he would be leaving this morning. I'd hoped he could at least spend his entire birthday weekend with me. At times I sweared Parlay had some other chick out there on the side. I mean, although I offered this man every sexual fantasy imaginable, he only wanted to sex me fifty percent of the time I wanted to sex him—So who's getting the other fifty? I didn't know, but I was gonna find out. I wouldn't be surprised if he was fucking Juicy on the low or if he started fucking Diamond. My brain raced with all sorts of crazy thoughts as I continued to clean.

I noticed Parlay's luggage neatly sitting in the corner of the bedroom, while he was downstairs waiting on his car to pick him up and take him to the airport. I tiptoed to the door and peeped out to make sure that he wasn't anywhere in sight. I then made my way back over to the luggage and stared at it. I could no longer resist the urge to search through it.

I unzipped his Gucci carry-on and started to sift through it. I wasn't sure what I was looking for, but I needed some sort of sign, something to give me an idea of what was going on. I'd changed so many aspects of my life for Parlay, I just refused to get played.

As I searched through his things, I came across condoms—That was strike one—What the hell did he need condoms for? I continued to search, but found nothing else suspect. I did, however, come across his itinerary. Luckily the flight was for him and his manager only. But just in case, I wanted to make copies of it.

Once again I tiptoed over to the door and peeked out. Seeing that the coast was clear, I rushed to the office and made a quick copy and then returned it back to its rightful place. I zipped his carry-on back up, folded up the itinerary, and then placed it in my pocket. That itinerary could certainly come in handy, because it provided both Parlay's flight information as well as his hotel information.

"C," Parlay yelled as he entered the room.

"Yeah, baby," I answered, trying to hide my anger.

"The car is here. I'm out. I'll be back in a couple of days." He kissed me on the lips and then headed out the door.

He didn't even bother thanking me for last night. Even this morning when he woke up, he never mentioned one thing about Diamond. Perhaps it wasn't memorable enough for him to bring up.

I definitely wasn't going to bring her up again. If Parlay was ever to get so lucky again, fuck Diamond, I was going for the cubic zirconia. I was the real deal, and the next bitch needed to know her place.

I walked over to the bedroom window that faced the driveway, separated the blinds with my hands and watched as Parlay jumped in the black Escalade with windows tinted so black, I could only see the reflection of his house in the window.

I turned around and leaned against the blinds. My head fell back, and I just looked up and sighed. I couldn't help wondering if his trip was a legit business trip or just some secret rendezvous.

I decided to go downstairs to make me a bite to eat. My eyes brightened up when I noticed his cell phone on the nightstand. The smile on my face was so wide that I thought my lips were going to split.

"Seems like Mr. Parlay was in such a hurry, he forgot all about his little cell phone," I said to myself aloud. "Looks like I'm about to get all my questions answered."

I picked up the phone and sat down on the edge of the bed. I continued to chat to myself as I searched through his phone. "Oh, we have a call from Juicy—strike two!" I yelled like a crazed umpire as I scrolled through his received calls.

Parlay had spoken to her today for exactly four minutes

and seventeen seconds. I had no idea they had even exchanged phone numbers. I'd been so focused on Diamond that I hadn't really paid much attention to Juicy. I should have known as soon as Parlay had the chance, that he would get at her. He'd been obsessed with her for months, with no means of getting her, and thanks to one birthday-night treat from me, I'd hooked up a deadly situation. And we all knew how deadly Ceazia Devereaux could get.

I continued to scroll through his numbers, but nothing else came up suspicious. Next, I searched through his cell phone address book. No suspicious females listed there, but that didn't prove anything.

Parlay wasn't the brightest bulb on the string of Christmas tree lights, but he wasn't the one that just won't shine and all, and keeps all the other ones from working. No, he wasn't just outright stupid at all.

Before ending my cell phone investigation, I noticed there were numerous saved numbers with no names. My woman's intuition warned me that those were the ones I should beware of. I grabbed a sheet of paper and wrote down every number in his phone that had no name attached.

Then I continued a couple last searches through his phone. I checked his pictures. Nothing too exciting there. And finally I checked his text messages. Still nothing. Now satisfied with my findings, I placed his phone back on the nightstand in its original spot, as though it had never been moved. I wondered how long it would take him to realize that he'd left his phone. I was even more curious to find out if he would come back for it.

I went back to my original task at hand; to prepare me something to eat.

After preparing a smoked turkey bagel sandwich, I poured me a glass of juice and moved to the living room and sat on the couch comfortably. I flipped through the channels. Although my favorite show, "What Not to Wear," was on, my mind was focused elsewhere. *What the hell is up with Parlay and Juicy? Maybe she could snatch him from underneath my nose. After all, I did do that to his last girlfriend. I've gotta find out what's up.*

It was eating me up inside. I had to know what was up with Parlay and Juicy. I couldn't call her though—that would be too obvious, and not my style at all. I'd never been a fan of the "insecure girlfriend" phone calls, so that optioned was out.

That's when it hit me. *Chastity! Why not call Chastity*? She, for one, should know Juicy's whereabouts. I mean, she was one of Bottoms Up's hottest commodities.

I grabbed my Sidekick, flipped it open, and scrolled to her number. I stared at it. I badly wanted to know if Juicy was working this weekend, but I was not trying to open an old wound. I'd put Chastity and the rest of the crew out my mind long ago and had been just fine without them. I didn't know if I was ready to face the music again. I had a new life now and wasn't trying to re-live the past.

I went back and forth with myself. It was as though I had

the devil on one shoulder and an angel on the other. Needless to say, like most of my battles, the devil won.

I called her up.

"This is Chastity." She answered the phone in her most professional voice.

My mind flashed back to the old days when we were back in Virginia. Chastity was always professional from her dress code to her "I'm-in-charge" voice. Always ready to get her big break, Chastity was the-college-grad-turned-entrepreneur.

"Hey, girl. This is C," I said in my phoniest tone.

"Oh. Hey, Ceazia. I wasn't expecting you to call," she said honestly.

"Well, I wasn't expecting to call either." I decided to be honest with her too.

"So what made you call?"

"Well, I was calling to ask you about one of your girls."

"Juicy?"

"And how did you know that?"

"Well, I can see from last night that you all had an added interest in her," she stated, still speaking in her professional tone.

"Yeah, I guess you could say that. So when is she working again? Is she on the schedule for the next few days?"

"Yeah, she is. Thursdays through Sundays are her busiest nights."

"Okay, great. That's what I needed to know."

"So you coming out? Maybe we can play catch-up. You know, there's a lot of things I want to chat with you about."

Chastity decided to drive down a one-way street, but she was headed in the wrong direction.

"Well, I'll give you a call and maybe we can chat over lunch," I lied.

"Okay, cool. Is this a good number for you?"

"Yeah." I really wanted to say no.

After speaking with Chastity, I could pretty much rule Juicy out. Now I had to find a way to make sure it wasn't Diamond. She made it a point to come off at me like she was "strictly-dickly," but I mean, after that stunt she and Parlay pulled last night, you would think they were long-time lovers.

Oh my God. What if they are? What if that whole department store hook-up was a set-up?

My mind began to race with all sorts of thoughts. I scrolled to her number in my cell phone and called her.

"Hi sexy," she answered her phone, sounding excited to hear from me.

"What's up?"

"So you calling for more?" she asked.

I wish I would let your trifling ass fuck my man again. I would have to kill your ass, bitch. "Uuuuummmmm, maybe."

"So what's up?"

"Nothing much. Just sitting here bored and alone. What do you have planned for the weekend?" I got straight to the point, just as I had done with Chastity.

"I was planning to spend some time at the dance studio, but other than that, nothing really—unless you had something in mind."

I wondered if that dance studio time was really Parlay time. I had to think of something fast.

"Well, why don't we spend the weekend together? That will give us some time to really get to know each other. Parlay is out of town for a couple of days, so it will just be me and you."

"Really? You really want to spend the weekend with me? This is the opportunity I've been waiting for. You won't be disappointed. When should I come over?" Diamond eagerly asked.

"How about now?"

Parlay was out of my sight, so I needed all prospects in sight, Diamond being one of them.

She agreed as expected. We ended the call with her promise of being at my doorstep within the next hour.

Now that I had all the prime suspects covered, I was in the clear to call Parlay.

At first, I accidentally called his cell phone that he had left here, but then I decided to call his other one. After just one ring it went straight to voice mail. I knew he wasn't on the plane already, so there was no reason for his phone to be off.

My brain began to race again. I couldn't bear to think this man could be cheating on me. I'd sacrificed too much for this relationship. I'd actually dropped the whole "street-saga-game idea" and tried to come straight. I could have been fuckin' a number of niggas and banking dough. And I hadn't even paper-chased or dug in this nigga's pockets, not once. And trust me, I'd had plenty of opportunities to run game on him and his niggas alike, but I'd made a promise to leave the sheisty life alone.

Damn, C! Shit! I amazed even myself. A bitch was on some real shit right now, but God forbid, Parlay reach strike three.

I'd done enough detective work of my own for the moment. But to ensure Parlay wasn't playing me, I decided it was time for a true private investigator to do a little detective work.

While waiting for Diamond's arrival, I grabbed my laptop and did a quick Internet search for Atlanta's top private investigators. After checking out the profile of a few, it didn't take long for me to find one I felt would be able to handle my job.

I wrote down all of their information and then called the office up. I needed background information on every muthafucka I was dealing with. I needed to know for certain what I was working with.

I felt as though the investigator had been hired to investigate me, with all the questions he was asking me, but he was just trying to get all of the information he possibly could, regarding the people I wanted him to investigate.

I told them exactly what I needed and who I needed it on. By the time our forty-minute conversation was over, I had equipped the investigator with a shitload of information—I'd provided Diamond's full name and phone number, as well as the information off of her modeling card; I gave them Juicy's place of employment and phone number.

Finally, I faxed them a copy of Parlay's itinerary. What

more could they ask for? If that didn't bring home the goods, then I didn't know what would.

"Ding-dong," the doorbell chimed like that of a huge mansion.

I knew it was Diamond. Her timing was perfect.

I logged off the computer and opened the door, having no idea what the weekend had in store for me. Although that little session we had last night was good, I was not up for a bunch of clit-licking and coochie-grinding all weekend. I just needed her here to make sure that she was not some place else with my man. So if that meant that I had to pretend a little, lie a little, and manipulate a little—hell, or even steal or kill a little—I would.

All in the name of love, ya heard! Never said better than my "Dirty South" niggas!

CHAPTER 11

Angel

"Bring out the gangster in me"

What a wonderful day. What more could I ask for? When I started out this morning, I had no idea that I was going to get this close to that trifling bitch, Danielle. After lunch with her fiancé, Richard, I practically had all the information I needed to ruin her life. But why stop there? I was interested in knowing what her little friend, Shawn, has up his sleeve.

I was thinking, it might be a little more enjoyable to work with him to bring down her little empire anyway. I searched through my purse to grab my cell phone. I figured I may as well give Shawn a call, since I was on such a roll.

"Yo," he answered.

"Hey, this is Angel. I met you earlier. You wanted to talk to me about Danielle," I said, trying to refresh his memory.

"Oh yeah. What's up?"

"I wanted to know if you wanted to get together today and talk. I just left her fiancé and I was able to get a lot of information from him. So I figured we could combine what we have and maybe come up with something."

"That's cool. Let's meet somewhere near the West End."

That was absolutely out of the question. "No can do," I quickly replied. That was definitely not my type of area to be hanging out at.

"What? You afraid to come on this side?" Shawn teased. "Scared of your own people?" He chuckled.

"Not at all, but I am not coming over there. We can meet in the city."

"That's cool. How about Justin's?"

"See you there in about thirty minutes."

In a matter of no time I was at the restaurant. I parked my car, and since I had a few minutes to spare, I returned a phone call from one of my clients. She'd just found out that her husband-to-be and his ex-wife had the same colors when they got married, and was now trying to change her color scheme only one month before the wedding. She was worried that some of the same guests at the husband's last wedding would think she was copying off his ex.

I was able to convince her of how childish that would be to change her dream wedding because of something as petty as that. Of course I was much more diplomatic.

After putting out that fire with a little spit, I went inside the restaurant. Shawn was nowhere in sight, but I didn't worry because it was still a little early.

I grabbed a seat at the bar as I waited on his arrival. "Be Without You," the sweet sound of Mary J. Blige, chimed through my cell phone.

"Hi, John," I answered, not too enthused.

"Hello, honey. How's your day?" He asked as though he was really concerned.

I started to ask him how his morning was in court, but I couldn't risk blowing my cover. "My day is just wonderful," I happily boasted, rolling my eyes in my head.

"Well, that's good. I was just checking on you—"

"Baby," I said, stopping him.

"Yes, baby."

"Did you think about what we discussed last night? Still no one in mind?" I asked, hoping to put the pressure on him. "I want to do this while it's fresh on my mind and I'm feeling like being a little risqué. I'm afraid if we procrastinate, then I may change my mind and it will never happen."

"Okay, Danielle, "I'll see what's up and let you know."

I knew he was fronting, so I pressured him even more. "Tonight, John. Let me know what's up tonight."

"Okay, all right, *Angel*," Jonathan replied and disconnected the call.

"Another dime in the bucket," I said, hanging up the call. I knew it was a matter of time before I'd have my husband and his mistress right where I needed them. I just had to continue to play my cards right—which is why I just let him get that one off—calling me by that bitch's name on the phone.

Now I had to get in Shawn's head and see where he was coming from, and soon things will be lined up perfectly.

"Angel," I heard someone say as I felt a tap on my shoulder.

I turned around to find Shawn standing there.

"Shawn?"

He confirmed with a nod.

"Let's grab a table." I walked from the bar toward the hostess. "Excuse me, Miss, we're ready to be seated at a table now."

She quickly sat us down, provided us with a menu, and took our drink orders.

I jumped right into things. "So, Shawn, tell me your story—What's your beef with Danielle?"

"A woman who wastes little time."

"Time is money."

"Then we're on the same page already."

I raised an eyebrow.

"I already told you, ma, my beef with Danielle is that she owes me a little something."

This was not going to work for me by far. I needed to know all details before I agreed to do anything with him, so that there would be no misunderstandings or game-playing, something I shared with him up front.

"Look, Shawn, I understand that you may have to abide by your little street code and can only tell so much of whatever it is that's going on between you and little Miss Danielle, but I'm not from the streets, honey. You're dealing with a professional woman who knows how to handle her business. I'm not going to be sloppy with anything I do.

All *I*'s will be dotted and all *T*'s will be crossed—you can trust me on that. So, if we're going to be working together, I need to know everything there is to know, so that I know what I am dealing with and what I can expect, feel me?"

"Ha-ha-ha!" He laughed hysterically. "Yeah, ma, I feel ya."

"Okay, great. So what's your story?"

"Listen carefully because I'm only going to tell this story once." He cleared his throat. "I know Danielle from years back. She lived in Virginia and dated this dude that used to cop from me—"

"Excuse me?—I need you to use English, honey. I'm not familiar with all this street slang."

He shook his head and sighed. "Okay, her man, Snake, was a dude that used to buy drugs from me. Well, he ended up getting murdered, leaving Danielle to have to fend for herself and on her own. Of course, she wasn't able to take care of herself and live the life she had been accustomed to."

He allowed his mind to wander off and reminisce for a moment. He shook his head. "Hell, she couldn't live at all. And you know me, like any man where I'm from would do, I took advantage of her situation. I snatched her up during her most vulnerable time, and we kicked it.

"I basically kept up that lifestyle she was used to and she kept me pleased. Then after a while she began to trip, being unruly and shit, so every now and then I had to discipline her.

"Things began to get worse and worse. It got to the point where I had to sleep with one eye open. Then out of nowhere the narcs were on my ass, and I ended up in jail.

"A month later, Danielle was nowhere to be found. It didn't take a genius to put all the shit together of how all of sudden, the narcs were on my ass. Bitch sold everything I owned and dipped, taking the money in my stash with her.

"I figured all along that Danielle had been setting me up." Shawn twisted his lips and nodded his head. "But when she disappeared like that, it confirmed things even more. Feds threw decades at a nigga, so that bitch thought she was home safe. I ended up getting out a lot sooner than anyone had expected, though.

"As soon as I hit the pavement, I did my homework and found out that she was working here in Atlanta at some big law firm, screwing her way to the top." He leaned back in his chair and sipped on his drink that the waitress had just sat down in front of him.

I followed suit and took a sip from mine, listening intensely.

"I've already paid her a visit to make my presence in the ATL known. Although everything in me wanted to ring that bitch's neck, I just let her know that all I need from her is my money, and all that other shit between us is squashed. I don't even care that she set me up. The fact is, I didn't even lead her on to know that I know, in my heart of hearts, that she's the one that set me up."

He leaned forward and stared into my eyes. "But like I

said, I ain't even on that shit. My main mission, ma, is to get my loot and get the hell on."

He leaned back in his chair and then took another sip of his drink. "Ahhh." He crossed his arms on the table. "So what's your deal?"

I took a moment before responding. I had to take in and situate all of the details of Shawn's story. He'd made a few comments that I thought needed a little elaboration before we moved on to me and my story.

"What do you mean, Danielle is screwing her way to the top?"

"Come on, now." Shawn sucked his teeth. "You may not be from the streets, but I know you know what the hell I mean by that. Think about it—she's engaged to an NBA star, Richard Anderson, and she's basically secured her next position as partner with the biggest law firm in Atlanta by fucking the shit out of one of the senior partners, this cat named Dario."

I took in every word Shawn was saying, but even with all that at hand, I couldn't understand what this bitch wanted with my man. *What the fuck could John offer her*? I got so caught up in the fact that she was somehow using John in one of her little schemes that would ultimately lead to the end of our marriage.

Tears began to fill my eyes. This bitch had everything. Was her life not good enough that she had to steal my little joy too?

"Come on, boo, I thought you was a soldier," Shawn said.

"You gotta be gangsta for this shit. You can't get on a mission to seek revenge and be crying and shit. I can't risk you wussin' out or crackin' under pressure and shit."

I picked up a napkin and wiped my eyes.

Just then the waitress came over to the table. She was prepared to take our orders, but then she saw that I was upset and looked over to Shawn.

He held his hand up, signaling to her to come back. "So what's it gonna be?" he said to me. "Turn that hurt into hate, ma."

I regained my composure and sat up straight. "All I want to know, Shawn, is—if Danielle is a woman who sounds as though she has everything, what does she need my man for?"

"It's simple—Danielle longs for attention and praise. That was the only missing element from her perfect little life. And that's where your husband steps in—He has nothing more but that needed compassion." Shawn explained as though he was Dr. Phil himself.

To me, Shawn's theory wasn't enough, but still he had provided the *tit*, so now it was my turn to *tat*.

"Okay, well here's my story. Basically, I suspected that John was cheating. Not to provide you with too much information, but I knew this when our sex life changed. He would often beg me to be a little more adventurous when it came to us having sex. That just wasn't me though, you know, so I would always decline. That didn't stop him from trying to persuade me though. I mean every night he had a

DVD or new toy or some sort of gel or cream for me to try, but I just wasn't into it. Then one day everything just stopped. No more nagging or begging about trying new things, toys, etcetera. Hell, he barely even asked for sex period. I knew then that the reason he wasn't nagging and begging anymore was because he didn't have to; someone was giving it to him willingly, without a fuss. I was bound and determined to find out just who she was.

"So I started by tracking his cellular bill," I continued. "That was my starting point. From there, I was able to obtain a name, and the rest is history, leading up to the present." I gave Shawn a serious look—"Leading up to the future."

"Are you ready to order now?"

"Oh, I'm sorry. Yes, we are." I quickly scanned the menu and ordered.

Shawn did the same.

"I'll be right back out with your orders." She took our menus and walked away.

Shawn and I continued our conversation.

"I used every connection I had to get any available public information I could on Danielle," I informed him. "Probably just like you did. But then I figured that if she was the one my husband was fucking, then sooner or later he'd lead me to her, and that's exactly what he did."

"Just like a man—I don't know what the fuck we be thinking. Guess we just be hypnotized by the scent of pussy and can't think straight."

"Can't think with anything other than your dicks is what

it is." I almost took my anger out on Shawn, like him and every other man on the planet was just alike. "Anyway, one day I followed John, and he led me to a condo that they use as their little love nest. I saw the two of them enter together like they were husband and wife—That was the final straw—At that point I vowed to destroy that bitch."

I waved down the waitress and asked for a glass of water because a bitch was on fire now. The more I talked about it, the angrier I got. Unfortunately, I had been holding all of this inside of me, and now telling Shawn was a form of release.

"I followed Danielle to the Atlantic Station Lofts. I checked out the place, but it was negative according to the information I had dug up on her. My conclusions were uneventful, but as I was going to my car, getting ready to leave, I ran into Mr. NBA, her husband-to-be."

"No shit?"

" 'No shit,' diarrhea, or piss. He was agitated because I was parked in his reserved spot. We had a couple of words, and that's when I found out that he was Danielle's fiancé."

"He just told you that shit?"

"Not just right out. Somehow the fact that he had a fiancée, and that her name was Danielle, came up. I knew what the odds were that he was speaking of the same Danielle I was looking for—damn good odds! Nonetheless, I gave him my business card, since I just happen to be a wedding planner."

"That nigga called?" Shawn said, full of his statement-like questions. "What about when he mentions your name to her?"

"I do business under my maiden name, so she'll never put it together—And, yep, he did call. We even had lunch together. I was able to gather a whole lot of information from him about our little, marked woman. Now I plan to put that, with what you know, to come up with the ultimate plot of revenge."

Shawn just sat there staring at me for a moment as I rubbed my hands together like a mad scientist.

"Yeah, ma, I think you gon' hold up just fine." He cracked a smile. "So, now that we got why we want this bitch so bad out of the way, let's talk about what we're going to do to get her. You seem to have all the brains—So what's our plan? They say a man can never go wrong with a combination of street-smarts and book-smarts."

I was slightly honored that Shawn seemed to be placing his confidence in me. I thought for a minute. "You want your money, and I want her whole world to cave in. I want to destroy everything she's worked to accomplish; but in order to do that, I have to get close to her. The closer I am, the easier it is to destroy her. She definitely doesn't need to know that you and I know each other, so don't even mention John's name to her. Definitely keep that quiet. Meanwhile, just keep putting the pressure on her about your money. Pretty soon I should be able to give you a little something to help persuade her a little more."

"Damn! I fuck with you, ma. You are kinda gangsta in a

high-class kinda way," Shawn said between laughter. "So once you get close to her, then what. Tell me, Angel—what's the end that's going to justify your means?"

A wicked smile spread across my lips as I proceeded to tell Shawn the details of what I had in mind as the ultimate plot for revenge.

Danielle thought her world might have crumbled before, but this time she'll be lucky to even have a life.

CHAPTER 12

Jonathan

"Three's a party"

Angel was really pressuring me about this threesome thing. It was almost to the point where I was starting to feel uncomfortable. I mean, she was starting to act like me. I couldn't understand it; how she and I had just completely flipped scripts. I'd tried to mention it before, and she stormed off into the bathroom and cut me off from sex for almost a week. Now all of a sudden, she's got this thing about pleasing her man. Maybe it was more of a fantasy for her than a moment of pleasure for me. But nonetheless, I was going to at least put forth the effort to make it happen. After all, what does a man have to lose when it comes to a threesome with his wife and his mistress?

I picked up the phone and dialed Danielle's phone number.

"Hello?"

"Hello, Danielle. How you feel?" I was hoping she would say, "Horny."

"Better. Much better. You know I called the doctor and you were exactly right—It *is* panic attacks. Evidently I'm stressing too much. I made an appointment to see a psychologist later in the week."

"Well, that's good. You've gotta take care of yourself. A beautiful woman like you shouldn't be so worried." I continued laying it on thick, icing her up with all the things I knew she wanted to hear. "Where are you now?"

"At the office."

"Baby, give yourself a break. Why don't we do dinner?" I figured after a few martinis would be the perfect opportunity to pop the "threesome question."

"I'll have to check. Richard is in town and he may have something planned for us—on second thought, fuck Richard—sure, we can have dinner. What time?"

I had no idea what was going on between her and Richard, but it seemed to be working out in my favor. "Let's say, seven."

"Perfect. See you then."

I hung up the phone curious as to what old Richard boy had done this time. If I had to guess, I would say that Danielle and Richard were in a fight because he'd rather be with the boys than spend time with her. Whether that was the deal or not, Richard had fucked up, and I was going to be there to take up the slack as usual. I was definitely going to use their little argument to my advantage.

"This may be Angel's lucky night after all." I picked up the phone and dialed her number.

"Baby, I have a candidate."

"That fast, huh?"

Her response confused me. "Huh? Baby, earlier you were saying I had to hurry and don't procrastinate or you may lose interest. Now you're saying, 'that fast.' Is this some sort of trick?"

"No, honey, not at all. I'm just surprised. Earlier you seemed sort of uncertain, and now look, you already have someone!" She paused for a minute.

"So who is it? Is it any of the ladies I've met?"

"No. Actually, it's one of my clients. I thought it would be awkward to have a threesome with someone in the office and have to see them every day," I lied.

"Oh, okay. So when will you know for certain whether she's game or not?"

"Well, that's what I was calling you about. I am taking her out to dinner tonight. I've already thrown the idea out there for her to think about. She didn't say no, which means she may be interested. She's never done anything like this before, so she wanted to talk to me about it a little more. I need you to be available around seven, just in case she wants you to meet us at dinner or if she decides to be down with it after dinner."

"Sounds like a plan. I'll await your call."

"You do that."

Seven o'clock rolled around in no time at all. I finished up a few things at the office then called Danielle and confirmed our meeting location. Of course, I allowed her to pick the place. She chose Houston's.

When I arrived at the restaurant, Danielle was already there. I walked up behind her and began to massage her shoulders. "We're going to release all that tension tonight. This will be your most relaxing and stress-free night in months." I kissed Danielle on the neck.

"Ah, that feels so good," she moaned as she allowed her head to rest forward.

I continued to massage her shoulders.

"You know your massages make me weak." She turned around and gave me a small kiss on the lips.

I put my hands around her waist and returned the kiss.

A few moments later, we were led to our table—Danielle had already signed in our names. Once seated, Danielle began to look over the menu.

I figured I had to be the one to start a conversation up.

"So is everything okay with you and Richard? I'm only asking because you seemed a little irritated with him earlier."

"No, everything's not okay. We had a huge fight, and I haven't spoken to him since." She hung her head low.

"Hey, hey, hey, none of that. You heard what I said when I came in—we are releasing tension, not stressing. Now what would you like to drink?—And I'm not talking about soda or tea—a real drink."

"How about a shot of Patron?" Danielle was quick to say.

I was shocked by her response, but that's exactly what I

wanted to hear. I ordered two shots right away, one for each of us.

Those shots were the icebreakers. Danielle was obviously much looser after that, more talkative and happy-go-lucky, but I still didn't want to make my move just yet.

"What are you eating?" I looked over my own menu.

Just then, the waitress walked over to our table. "Are you both ready to order?" She looked back and forth from me to Danielle.

"You ready, honey?" I asked Danielle.

"Sure."

We ordered a couple of appetizers before ordering our main course.

Then we ordered more drinks; an apple martini for her and a Heineken for me. I didn't mind her being fucked up, but I needed to be fully aware of all that was going on.

Once our appetizers arrived, I still hadn't mentioned the threesome to Danielle. Between her throwing drinks back one after the other, I didn't know if there'd be room for conversation anyhow. Besides, I figured the more she drank, the more she'd be apt to agree to the threesome.

"Excuse me." Danielle flagged down the waitress. "Could the gentleman and I have another shot of Patron?" she asked with a drunken giggle.

Three shots of Patron and a Heineken later, I was a bit tipsy myself. I made sure the waitress kept my water glass full, though, to flush out the alcohol.

In-between bites of our entrée, Danielle and I found ourselves talking and laughing constantly, but about what, I had no idea. Every little thing done or said was hilarious to her. Watching her act in such a manner was hilarious to me.

I looked at my watch and noticed the time. It was already nine o'clock. Time had slipped away. I excused myself and took a trip to the restroom. On my way back to the table, I thought to check my cell phone because I had turned the volume down before going in the restaurant to meet Danielle.

I had five missed calls, all of them from Angel. "Damn," I said to myself under my breath. "I knew she was going to snap. Her mind was probably going nuts. It was bad enough that I was out to dinner with the girl who was the prospective third party to our threesome, and now I wasn't answering my cell phone. I could only imagine what was going through her mind. She probably thought that I was testing out the merchandise.

I made a U-turn and headed back to the restroom to give her a call. Her phone rang, but there was no answer. I waited a few seconds and tried her again, but it went to voice mail.

After a third strike, I was out; headed back to the table to join Danielle. I figured I would wrap things up and try calling Angel as I left out the restaurant.

As I headed toward the table, I noticed another young lady speaking to Danielle. They were chatting as if they were old friends. As I got closer, my drunken eyes cleared. "Shit! What the fuck!" I said out loud.

They both turned their heads in my direction.

"Oh you're back. I thought you had fallen in," Danielle joked.

"Hi, honey." Angel walked over to me and gave me a hug. "I'll take it from here," she whispered in my ear. She then pulled her head back, winked at me, and kissed me on the lips.

My heart raced as I sat at the table with my wife and my mistress. I hoped and prayed Angel knew what the fuck she was doing.

God, don't let Danielle say the wrong thing.

The last thing I needed was for Angel to find out that I had been sleeping with Danielle. This night was not working out according to plan. The last thing I wanted was for Angel and Danielle to be involved in casual conversation—That's how things tend to slip out, and with Danielle in her drunken state, Lord only knows what could happen.

"So, Danielle, I'm sure my husband has mentioned our little fantasy to you." Angel didn't bat an eye, as she sat down in the chair next to Danielle.

My mouth nearly hit the floor as I watched the circus before me. I needed another drink, but declined the waitress' offer when she came over to the table. I needed to be levelheaded now, more than ever.

"Yeah, he did. But I–I don't know just how I feel about all that yet," Danielle slurred. "I've never done anything like that before. You know, it's not every day a girl gets an invitation to join a husband and wife in a threesome. Then again, in this day and age—" Danielle giggled. "But anyway, I just don't know."

"Oh," Angel said, scooting her chair over close to Danielle's, "that's a disappointment." Angel began to rub Danielle's thigh. "I was really looking forward to it, Danielle, and now that I've seen you, I was starting to look forward to it even more." She moved closer to Danielle's inner thigh.

My mouth was hanging open. I couldn't believe this was my wife sitting in front of me. I couldn't help but wonder if Angel had, had a few herself before arriving. I had never seen her with this much courage before.

From the look on Danielle's red, drunken face, I could tell she was actually enjoying the attention she was receiving from Angel. It looked as though all my efforts had been in vain the way she just swooped right in and took control. This wasn't my wife. No, not the same "I-don't-suck-dick, don't-go-near-my-ass—no-that's-gross" woman.

Just seeing her in action made my dick rise. I discreetly slid my hand under the table and began to massage my erect penis. I continued to watch Angel work her magic on Danielle.

"I've never done anything like a threesome either," Angel confessed. "You can ask my husband. I haven't done much of anything, but all that is about to change."

"You sound as though you have a few tricks up your sleeve." Danielle raised her eyebrows at Angel.

"I just might." Angel lifted her hand from Danielle's thigh. "And you look like you could probably teach me some new ones."

Angel took her index finger and thumb and picked the

cherry off of the toothpick that Danielle had taken out of one of her drinks and laid on the table. "What tricks can you do with this?" She dangled the cherry in Danielle's face.

"Mmmmm . . . I think I could think of a few things," Danielle responded, now totally captivated by my wife's sensuality.

"Let's see."

Danielle stuck out her tongue and began to slowly lick all over the cherry. She flicked it and teased it with the tip of her tongue.

My eyes grew as I watched Danielle continue to molest the cherry.

Angel began rubbing Danielle's thigh once again. The both of them were tripping.

This shit is crazy.

Danielle used her entire mouth to inhale the cherry from between Angel's fingers, making sure she sucked on the tip of Angel's fingers in the process. Once the cherry, along with its stem was completely hidden in side Danielle's mouth, she smiled a seductive smile at Angel. She then opened her mouth, where the cherry was sitting at attention, like her tongue was the whipped cream on a sundae.

Danielle took her index finger and thumb and removed the cherry from her mouth. "Now it's your turn." She swung the cherry in front of Angel.

I took a deep breath as I waited for Angel's response.

"I don't think I can compete with you, but I think my

tongue action may be somewhat a little pleasing. But I'll let you be the judge of that." Angel's slowly licked the bottom of the cherry back and forth.

I monitored Danielle's reactions. She had the most erotic look in her eyes as she watched Angel's tongue maneuver about the same cherry, hitting the same spots her tongue had just hit.

Out of nowhere, Angel bites into the cherry, and some juice squirted onto Danielle's hand. Angel gently took her hand and licked it off, and chewed the remains of the cherry.

That was it. I'd seen enough. It was time to take this to the crib. My dick couldn't stand to be teased any longer.

"Okay, ladies, let's wrap this up." I then signaled for the waitress to come over to our table.

The ladies continued to entertain themselves in every way imaginable. They did every possible thing, short of tonguing each other down right there in the middle of the restaurant.

Once the waitress arrived at our table, I paid the bill and left her a healthy tip. It was her lucky night. I was overjoyed with what was about to go down, and she just happened to benefit from my gratitude.

We all stood up and headed out the door. I felt as though everyone around us knew that we were going home to have a threesome. As silly and as arrogant as it may sound, I felt proud. I straightened my back and walked a little taller than usual. I then grabbed their hands, one on either side of me, and guided them through the door.

Once outside, we began to scramble for car keys. There

was no way I could break up this party by allowing us each to go our separate ways. In addition to that, there was no way I could let Danielle drive. Not only was she in no condition to drive, I was afraid that if she parted from us and was on her own, she'd have time to realize what she was about to do and change her mind.

"Hold on, Danielle." I grabbed her by the wrist. "I know you don't actually think you are driving. Hand over the keys." I took the keys from her hand. "You can roll with me."

I noticed a dart from Angel when I made that statement, clearly notifying me of her disapproval.

"On second thought, why don't you ride with Angel, and I'll follow behind you ladies."

"Yes, Danielle," Angel said, taking her by the hand, "why don't you ride me—I'm sorry—with me."

Damn! I suddenly thought. *What if the two of them decide to finger each other or something, play with each other's clits and cum? Then where will that leave me?*

I packed up my selfish thoughts and headed for my car.

Angel had a closer spot than me, so she and Danielle hopped in her car. As I finally reached my car and hopped in, once I started it up, naturally I wanted to head straight to the condo I had rented for me and Danielle's secret rendezvous, but how would I explain that one to Angel? Although I knew that everything was pretty much engraved in stone to go down tonight, I still didn't feel quite that comfortable bringing Danielle to my home. Hard dick or not, something just didn't sit well with me on that one.

I took out my cell phone and dialed Angel.

After two rings she picked up. "Yes, John."

"Babe, I was thinking we should get a hotel room."

"For what, John?" Angel asked in a peculiar tone.

Thanks to the alcohol, my senses weren't one hundred percent yet, and I couldn't think of a lie quick enough. "I don't know. Forget it. Go ahead to the house." I hung up.

Since I had no valid reason to give Angel, I had no other choice but to just leave things alone. I didn't want to make it an issue and have her question my skepticism.

After about a ten-minute drive, I was pulling into the driveway behind Angel. *There's no turning back now.* I stepped out of my car and followed the ladies into my home.

Just as soon as I unlocked the front door and the two women were inside, they began tonguing each other down. They were passionately rubbing their hands in each other's hair. There went my dick again, damn near busting out the zipper of my pants.

"You and that tongue of yours," Angel said to Danielle as they each put their tongues back in their own mouths. "Come on, let's go, you two."

Angel looked over at me and then at Danielle and signaled us to follow her, with a nod of her head. She led us up the steps and into our master bedroom, like she was the mother goose and we were the goslings. Once in the bedroom, Angel went to the attached master bath and turned on the water to the Jacuzzi.

"You wanna come stick your hand in it to make sure it's

warm enough?" Angel looked at Danielle and licked her lips.

Danielle bit her bottom lip and made her way over to the Jacuzzi.

Angel moved out of her way, allowing her to bend over and test the water.

I whispered into Angel's ear, "Aren't you afraid getting in the Jacuzzi will sober her up?"

"John, she's pissy drunk. I don't want a damn date rape charge. Plus, the bitch is one step away from being partner at Atlanta's biggest damn law firm! We would be underneath the jail."

Danielle stood up and waved the water droplets from her hand. "Feels real good," she said to Angel. "I can't wait to get all up in it."

I don't mean to sound invisible, but I felt jealous. I was the one Danielle had been fucking for almost a year now, not Angel. I guess new pussy excites a motherfucker, no matter if they are a man or a woman.

"Good." Angel began to gather scented bath beads, bath salts and every other womanly bath product known to man. She then walked over to me and placed her hands on my chest. "Why don't you make yourself useful and set the bedroom up? Make it a little romantic."

I obeyed my wife's orders as she turned her attention back towards Danielle. I could hear them in there, giggling and laughing together as I lit some incense. The thought of Angel wanting this more for herself than for my enjoyment crossed my mind once more. *I guess the true test will be when the action goes down in bed tonight.*

I turned on some music, lit some candles, and brought out all the toys, lotions, oils, and sex games I'd unsuccessfully tried to get Angel to use. Hell, I figured tonight may be the only opportunity to get to use them, so why not bring them all out?

Just as I finished setting up things in the bedroom, Danielle and Angel walked in, draped in nothing but open robes. Angel was wearing the long burgundy and black satin, oriental-looking one that she always looked so delicious in, and Danielle was looking pretty edible herself in one of Angel's other robes, an all-black poly and cotton number that fell to her lower thighs.

"Wow! You ladies are beautiful." The words flowed from my mouth on impulse. I slowly sat down on the bed in awe, my eyes making love to the vision before me.

Their smiles showed that they appreciated my flattering comments. Each of them sat down beside me on the bed.

Any other time I would have pounced on them like a kangaroo, but of all the moments in the world, of all the situations I'd ever found myself in, I picked this one to freeze up. I absolutely felt paralyzed. I just sat on the bed; a stupid grin on my face.

I tried giving myself a little pep talk. *What the fuck are you doing, John? Get yourself together. This is the best fucking night of your life.*

"John?" Danielle placed her hand on my crotch and whispered my name.

I nearly jumped off the bed. "Yeah," I said, trying to breathe normally. I felt like I had caught one of her anxiety attacks.

"Are you okay, honey? Is this too much for you?" Angel began to rub my back.

Before I could answer, Danielle was undoing my pants.

"No, I'm fine. Are you ladies okay? Danielle, are you sobered up a little? Everybody fine with this decision?" I asked, attempting to direct the attention elsewhere. I couldn't believe I was stalling.

"Oh, that's what you're worried about?" Danielle directed me to stand up. She pulled my pants down.

I kicked my shoes off and stepped out of the pants.

"John, it's okay. I'm comfortable with it." Danielle softly pushed me back down on the bed.

Angel then proceeded to take off my shirt.

"Angel told me all about you being worried that I may feel as though you are taking advantage of me because I might have had one too many. But trust me, I assure you that I am well aware of everything. But that was so thoughtful of you."

I shot a look at Angel as if to say, "Why you lie?"

Danielle caught the look, but I don't think she realized what it was for. "Here." She dropped one of her arms down to her side and then held the other one out. "Give me some paper."

"Huh?" I asked.

"Give me a pen and a piece of paper."

"Right there." I pointed. "In the side table drawer."

Danielle pulled out a pen and a piece of paper from the tablet that was inside the drawer and proceeded to write.

I looked up at Angel, who had a puzzled look on her face. She just shrugged her shoulders.

"There, here you go." Danielle dropped the pen on the side table and handed me the piece of paper. "Go ahead, read it out loud," she said as I sat there holding it.

I read the letter aloud. "*I, Danielle ——, willfully agree to engage in a ménage à trois, also known as a threesome, with Mr. and Mrs. Jonathan Powell on this night, April 19, 2006. Signed and dated by Danielle ——.*"

"Now, how's that?—a signed document that will stand in the court of law." Danielle took the note from my hands and laid it on top of the pen.

Well, that fixed any of Angel's worries that she so freely blamed on me.

"Well, now that we're past that stage, let's have some fun. We can start by playing sexual dice." I was determined to put each one of my pleasure toys into action, especially after the obscene amount of money I had spent on them.

I pulled out the pair of dice. One read *kiss*, *blow*, *suck* and *touch*; the other read *nipple*, *butt*, *lips*, *clit*.

"Who's first?" I shook the dice and blew on them like I was playing a game of cee-lo.

"I'll go first." Danielle took the dice from me and rolled them—*lick nipple*—So whose nipple do I lick?"

"The both of ours," Angel was quick to say—"John, get naked—" Angel pointed to my boxers and socks.

As I undressed, Danielle removed Angel's robe and then gently pushed her onto the bed and began to slowly lick her nipples one by one.

When she looked up and noticed that I was completely undressed, she used her index finger to signal for me to come join them on the bed.

As soon as I sat down, she pushed me back and began doing the same thing to me that she had been doing to Angel.

I began to moan with pleasure as Danielle clinched my nipple tenderly between her lips, hardening them like old Play Dough. Although this was nothing new for me, with Danielle it was much more pleasurable. This time it wasn't on the DL, with the fear of getting busted; it was open and free.

Next, it was Angel's turn to roll. She picked up the dice and rolled—*kiss lips*.

"Awwww, that is way too simple!" Danielle yelled.

Angel grabbed Danielle by the face and tongued her down. She then turned to me and gave me a small seductive kiss.

Finally it was my turn at the dice. I shook them and rolled—*blow clit. How appropriate*!

"Whew!!!!! Big money!" Danielle screamed, obviously still buzzing off her liquor high.

"So where do I start?" I directed my question to Angel, looking at both ladies.

"Here." Angel slid the robe off Danielle and pushed her to her back and spread her legs.

"Yeah, right here, baby—" Danielle pulled her neatly shaved lips apart and gave her pussy a few gentle pats.

Nothing left to do but my business, I dived in tongue first.

"Wait!" Danielle grabbed my head and pushed me away. "This is a night to remember—pull out the video recorder."

The shock on Angel's face looked like, "Why didn't I think of that?"

Without hesitation, I pulled out our two-in-one digital camera and set it up. I then went back over to the bed, where Danielle had been keeping her pussy warm by rubbing on it.

"Now let's get down to business," Danielle said as she forced my head back to the position I was in before.

I licked her vagina cautiously. I tried to please Danielle and provide a little action for the camera, and at the same time, avoid angering Angel.

As I sent Danielle to the moon, Angel grabbed the tube of pleasure liquid and placed some on Danielle's nipples. The application was simple—rub, blow, lick. Those three simple actions would cause a heating sensation on the nipples and then a quick cooling, resulting in an instant increase in the already warming sensation.

Danielle began to moan for the next few minutes. I licked her pussy like I was a dog and she was my feeding bowl. I sucked on her clit, licked her clit, and plunged my tongue in and out of her pussy until she was fucking my face.

Meanwhile, Angel was treating her nipples like Tootsie

Roll Pops, making sure her tongue gave each nipple an equal amount of attention.

The game of sexual dice became no more—we tested every, toy, cream, and oil, as well as ventured to every part of each other's bodies with our tongues and fingers, Angel conducting us each, every step of the way.

I must say that I was truly pleased, to say the least.

When that part of the fun was over, Angel poured us each a glass of wine, I suppose to keep our minds in the game.

We drank the wine from each other's glasses and tongues until finally it was time to fuck.

Angel laid me down in the middle of the bed, and her and Danielle lay on each side of me. Danielle began kissing me as Angel massaged my dick, nutsack and all. I could feel the each of them squirming and grinding on my leg, the wetness and warmth of their pussies making me moan.

I cupped their asses and squeezed, making sure not to do any more to Danielle than to Angel. The last thing I wanted was for the needle to get pulled off the record and the party to be over.

My fingers traveled to their pussies and entered them.

They moaned and flexed their pussies around my fingers.

In and out I pleased them. The faster I went, the more passionate Danielle kissed me and the faster Angel stroked my dick.

It didn't take long for both women to want the dick.

Of course, Angel was quicker to the draw. She hopped on

me and slid down my dick like a porno star, and began popping her pussy.

"Ummm." Danielle took her finger and began fondling Angel's clit.

Feeling the sensation deep within of my dick hitting her spot and Danielle plucking at her clit, Angel's juices poured out. She collapsed on my chest.

Danielle couldn't wait to get hers. With Angel still laying on me, Danielle scooted her up by the ass so that my dick was accessible. She then stuffed my dick inside of her and began fucking me like crazy, banging into Angel, making it look like she was getting fucked too.

"Oh shit." Angel flinched and closed her eyes.

I knew right then that Danielle was fingering Angel while I was fucking.

"You like this, baby?" I asked her.

"Yes." Angel began kissing me.

I grabbed her by the head and shoved my tongue down her throat while Danielle fucked me so hard that the bed was banging into the wall.

Angel began panting as Danielle finger-fucked her.

Then Danielle said those four little words that just set us all off—"I'm about to cum," she panted.

It was then that we all put our backs into it, intermingling our juices, climaxing in sequences. Danielle then collapsed on Angel's back. The feeling, words can't explain . . . words can't explain.

Once Danielle got up, she poured us each another glass of wine. "Just what I need to take the edge off." She said, sounding much more sober now. She sipped some of her wine and let out a refreshing, "Aaahhh."

I was much more concerned with Danielle leaving than her "taking the edge off." Our work here was done, so we needed to wrap this little episode up and move out. I was glad it happened, and now I was even happier that it was over.

"We've gotta get you to your car," I reminded.

"Yeah, you're right. I'll call a cab."

"Oh no, you won't. I'll take you."

"Well, thank you." Danielle gazed at Angel. "Angel, you are a beautiful person. I've never met anyone so sweet. Are you sure it's not a problem?—It's awfully late."

"I won't have it no other way."

Feeling obligated, I offered to ride along, but Angel turned me away, saying she wanted it to be girls' time.

I couldn't argue with that one.

I saw them off then headed to bathroom. I took a hot shower, changed the sheets on the bed, and in a matter of seconds, was off to sleep.

I was startled when I felt a small shake on my shoulder.

"John, John, wake up," Angel whispered.

"Yeah, baby. What is it?" I said with a stretch and a yawn.

"I really like her. She's a nice woman—I thought you said she was one of your clients?"

The twenty-one questions are about to begin. "No. I met her through one of my clients," I lied. I yawned again and then closed my eyes.

"Oh, okay. She offered me a job, you know."

" 'Job'?" I turned over to face her.

"Yeah. She said once she gets her position as partner at the law firm she works for that she'll need a paralegal, and that she would love to have me."

"But, Angel, you know nothing about that line of work. And what about your wedding planning?"

"She said she would train me and that she was sure that I'd catch on quickly. I really think this is something I can do along with my wedding planning; it's extra income."

"I don't think it's a good idea, Angel. We're not trying to make this woman a permanent part of our lives—that's just too close for comfort."

"I disagree, but we'll talk more about it tomorrow. Good night." Angel kissed me on the check and then fell fast asleep.

I, on the other hand, couldn't get back to sleep if I wanted to. I tossed and turned for the rest of the night. The thought of Angel and Danielle working together kept me awake. I started to call Danielle and ask her what the hell was on her biscuit—what type of dumb move was that to offer my wife a job? How the hell were we supposed to have a down-low relationship, when my wife would be the one taking her messages from me?—There was no way this was going to work.

I turned on the television to clear my brain, so I could finally get some sleep, and eventually it did work. An hour later the TV was watching me. I was finally off to sleep, hoping that when I woke up, I would find that my conversation with Angel was nothing more than a nightmare.

CHAPTER 13

Danielle

"Steps away from the finish line"

My head was pounding as I struggled to put the keys in my front door. The effect of the combination of shots of Patron, Martinis, and wine had finally caught up with me.

When I finally got the door open, I rushed to the bathroom, dropping my clothes on the way, and "prayed to the porcelain god." I hadn't felt this way in years. I vomited so much that I had to have thrown up everything I'd eaten for the past two days. There was absolutely nothing else left to come out.

I drug myself from the toilet over to the bathtub, and flopped down into the empty bathtub. I turned the water on and filled the garden tub as high as I could without overflowing it, and then I turned on the jets. I laid my head on my bath pillow and relaxed.

As I enjoyed my moment of relaxation, I reminisced over the events of the night. I couldn't believe I'd actually had a threesome. I had never even considered such a thing, and in one night I actually did it.

And to top things off, I enjoyed it. It was so much fun . . . although I don't think I would've had the guts to do it if I had been sober. Well, good thing I'd gotten that out of the way before marriage.

As I lay there in the tub, my thoughts moved to Angel. *What a sweet woman*. I had no idea she would be so likeable. She was totally opposite from what I expected. The way Jonathan talked about her all this time, you would think she was just some boring homebody that liked to nag and gossip with the ladies. She so wasn't like that at all.

I wondered what would make Jonathan cheat with me on someone as sweet as her. I know I could be a stone cold bitch sometimes, but Angel didn't seem like she had a mean bone in her body. She seemed like the kind of wife men dream of. I truly surprised myself by taking to her in just that little bit of time we'd spent together.

On the ride from the restaurant to her house, she really opened up to me. She told me how she and Jonathan had been dating since she was eighteen, and that she was a virgin when they met. She thought her husband resented her because of her lack of sexual experience; one reason why she wanted to give him a threesome. She also went on to say how her husband felt her wedding planning business wasn't bringing in enough revenue so, to compensate, she'd been trying to get a second job.

Something in me just had to offer her the position as my paralegal after hearing her story. I guess I saw it as my way to repent for what I had been doing with her husband behind her back. I'd never really had any female friends, but if the day ever came that I did, I'd love to have had one like Angel.

The more I thought about Angel, the more guilt I began to feel for having a relationship with Jonathan. How could I ruin such a happy marriage? Angel didn't deserve this. Jonathan was loving, sweet, and thoughtful. She deserved to have her man to herself.

Tears began to well up in my eyes as I realized what I had to do—I had to leave Jonathan. In a few months I was going to be married myself. How would I feel if some woman came and took the man I loved so? I'd made a terrible, terrible decision, and I had to correct it. I wanted to call Jonathan right away, but I knew it was too late.

I decided to call him first thing in the morning. I stepped from the tub and prepared for bed. Before I got in bed, I got on my knees and prayed.

"God, I know I am not the spiritual person, but this is one time I need You. I realize what I have done is wrong, Lord, and I need to correct it. I beg for Your strength and guidance with this situation. In Jesus name, I pray. Amen."

It wasn't often that I called on God, but I knew He was the only one that could help me now. My prayers said, I hopped in my warm bed and turned on the television.

"Bang! Bang! Bang!" There was a huge knock on my front door.

Not again. I was sure it was Shawn here to torment me again. I took my time walking to the door. This time I headed to my newly installed back door first. No one was there.

"Bang! Bang! Bang!"

"I'm coming." I headed to the front door. I peeped out the hole and was shocked to see Richard. I opened the door right away.

"Why the fuck you ain't been answering yo' phone, Danielle?" He forced his way through the door.

"Richard, I don't even know where my phone is. And why are you here banging on my door in the middle of the night?" I asked calmly.

"I've been fucking calling you all day!" he continued to yell.

"Don't talk to me like that, Richard. I am not a child!"

I walked back into my bedroom, closing the door behind me. I had a long night and was too tired for the bullshit.

Moments later, I was off to sleep.

I was awakened by the bright sun, which shone through the bedroom blinds. The clock said 8:00 a.m.

I got up and walked into the living room, expecting to see Richard lying across the sofa fast asleep, but there was no sign of him.

It seemed the closer we got to the wedding, the further apart Richard and I had become. Every other day we were arguing; and it was usually about my focus on becoming partner at the firm, and not getting pregnant.

* * *

After a long day in court, I returned home hoping that I didn't have to armor up for another battle with Richard.

As I made my way up to the bedroom, there was no sign that he had even been home. I opened the bedroom door and soon noticed a sign of Richard—a note on the bed.

I picked it up and began reading it:

I already have a demanding career and it seems that you've become more and more involved in yours. This is slowly causing an enormous strain on our relationship. Although it was supposed to be a surprise, I've taken the liberty of planning our wedding. This should give you the time needed to concentrate on your career. Once your new position is obtained and you are all settled in, I hope you are able to put more time into perfecting our relationship. Until then, I'm stepping away. Maybe this will relieve some of the stress that you are under. Eventually the time will come when you will have to decide; your career or a family. Hopefully you will make the right decision. Take care.
Richard

I was blown by his letter, unsure how to take it. I wasn't sure if he was leaving me or just giving me the space necessary for my success. It's sad to say, but I was sort of glad he'd left this letter. I loved Richard and wanted to get married too, but right now my number one priority was my career.

With Richard out the way, I could finally focus on that and not worry about planning the wedding or having a child. I guess you could say it was a blessing in disguise.

I was amazed at how so many things could change for the better in a matter of only a few weeks. As days passed, I heard nothing from Shawn, less and less of Richard and Jonathan, and more and more of Angel and Dario.

After taking on that big case and winning it, without collapsing in the damn courtroom, I finally received my promotion as partner. I thought life would be perfect.

I'd stop having the panic attacks, I had no constant pressure from Richard to have a baby, and I was finally at a point in my career that I could tell Dario to kiss my ass.

Richard had finally given me a break, but Dario stepped in and became an even bigger headache than Richard ever was. Our little fling had obviously gotten the best of him, and he was on some shit now. I mean, completely whipped.

Just when I decided to cut Dario off, he decides that he's fuckin' in love with me and wants to have a relationship. Of course, that wasn't an option.

I caressed his big, fat face as we sat on the couch in his house. I was ecstatic inside. I knew this would be the last time I'd ever have to touch this man again, but still, I had to hide my excitement and play my role.

"Dario, sweetie, you've known from the beginning about Richard, and our wedding date is coming up soon."

"I know, but that was then. This is now—I had no idea

my feelings for you were going to develop into what it is now."

"Dario, please don't make this any harder for me than it is now." I lowered my head for effect. "I really can't handle this right now. You know how much making partner means to me. I'm already having a hard time balancing things out. Please don't add onto it. Not now."

He looked so fucking pitiful sitting there, eating up every last bite of my lies; I felt obligated to add a helping of false hope to his plate.

"Who knows what the future holds, but right now, I have to stay focused. Just let me get comfortable in my position and marriage. Things could change."

"Danny," he whined, "only because I care about you so much, I respect your feelings. The last thing I want to do is pressure you." He put his hand on top of mine and looked into my eyes.

I could have sworn I saw a tear well up in his eye. *I swear to God, if this big, black nigga cries, I 'm gonna smack him across his fat face.* This shit was becoming comical. I felt like I was in a heterosexual version of *Broke Back Mountain*.

If the next words out of Dario's mouth were, "I just don't know how to break up with you." It was gonna be over for me.

"Just knowing that the future may hold something for the two of us is enough to keep me going." He leaned in and stuck his disgusting tongue in my mouth.

Now that he had nothing that I needed, some things were just unimaginable—and having break-up sex was one of them. I quickly pulled away and stood up. I looked down at my watch. "Well, I gotta go now. I have a late appointment with a client just to go over some questions on the deposition."

He stood up to walk me to the door. "I'm gonna miss you, Danielle."

I chuckled. "Dario, we work together every day."

"You know what I mean—I'm gonna miss you in the sense of being with you; making love to you."

Although I had easily told many lies in my lifetime, I damn near had to pry this one from between my lips. "I'm gonna miss making love to you too." I started towards the door.

Dario stood up and followed. "You sure you don't have five minutes to spare?" Dario chuckled mischievously.

I turned around and squeezed his cheek. "Not even two minutes." I then made my way out of the door. I turned and waved at Dario, who was watching me walk away like some ol' big bitch.

I smiled the entire time I walked to my car. I unlocked the door and gave him a wink as I got in and pulled off.

After I stood up to Dario and told him we could have nothing more, I knew he would be a man of his word and respect my wishes.

Even though there were several occasions at the office when he would be an asshole, I still remained cordial with him. I mean, it wasn't anything serious he was doing to me. Just small things like trying to make an example out of me at meetings and increase my workload; giving me the extra shit that no one wanted.

But since I'd hired Angel as my assistant, she happily took the liberty of working on all the extra shit he piled on me.

Thank God for Angel. She'd become the closest thing I had to a friend. Not quite qualified as a paralegal, I hired her as an assistant instead. Either way, Angel was happy to be employed, and it showed through her work.

Now a co-worker and friend, Angel and I were nearly inseparable. The guilt about being with Jonathan began to bother me even more. I'd made my mind up. It was time to cut off any further sexual relations with Jonathan.

Since the night of our threesome, I had been avoiding Jonathan and distancing myself from him, but I had never really taken the time to just really cut things off. I felt that time had come. It was time for him to go, and for me to tell Angel the truth.

With every ounce of my soul I hoped that Angel could find it somewhere in her heart to forgive me. If not, losing her as a friend, and possibly an employee, would be the sacrifice. But I figured since things were finally starting to fall in order in my life, I may as well straighten this thing out too.

With Jonathan and Dario out of my life, my issues of infidelity would be resolved. Now my only focus would be my career and my new husband. I finally had control, and things were surely going my way. I'd worked long and hard for each step I'd progressed, and now that I was only moments away from the top, no one was going to take this away from me!

CHAPTER 14

Ceazia

"Gangster for life"

It had taken several weeks, much longer than I had expected, but the time had finally come. It was time to meet with the private investigator and find out just what the fuck Parlay had been up to. Today would be the moment of truth.

As the days had passed, I had gone on as normal, never giving Parlay the slightest clue that I thought he was messing around on me. I still loved him and continued to pamper him and give him the same treatment as always. After all, it hadn't been proven that he was cheating, so I still gave him the benefit of the doubt.

I watched the clock as the time counted down to my 10:00 a.m. meeting with the investigator. I had been up all morning, because I was so restless the night before, tossing and turning. Come 9:15, I could no longer bear the pressure. I grabbed my purse and keys and headed out the door to the Barnes and Noble Starbucks in Buckhead.

All sorts of things ran through my mind as I drove to my destination. I thought about who it was, or if it was more than one chick. I even played out in my head how I would react if I found out that Parlay was playing me to kick it with Diamond, after all.

Diamond and I had become rather close over the past few weeks, almost to the point where I would rule her out, but I didn't put nothing past no bitch. Although there were a few instances where I was not able to locate neither Diamond or Parlay at the same time, I knew that it could have been a coincidence. Besides, it's virtually impossible to know anyone's every move.

But like they say, "It only takes a minute to cheat."

Of course, I arrived at my destination a little early. I took a seat at a table by the window and watched for the investigator to show up. I sat at the table, tapping my foot and twirling my thumbs. I was too antsy to even order anything.

The anxiety was overwhelming. I didn't smoke, but that was one time I felt like I needed a cigarette—Black and Mild, clove or something.

"Whew! Thank God." I noticed the investigator walking up. I stood up and flagged him down as he entered Barnes and Noble.

He approached the table.

"I thought you would never get here." I extended my hand to greet the old, shabby-looking white man.

"Good morning, Ms. Devereaux." He grabbed a seat.

I took a deep breath and encouraged him to get right down to business. "So what have we got?"

"Well, before we get into the details of my findings," he started, "let me explain a few things." He pulled a folder out of his briefcase and placed it on the table. He then laid his arms across it. "First, I don't normally like to do the 'cheating investigating,' because it's so intense. I've had quite a few bad experiences, so to protect myself, as well as others, I limit the information I give."

His last line went in one ear and right out the other. Unless he was going to limit his fee, he was going to tell me every damn thing he had uncovered.

"Now, let me give you the details of my investigation." He unfolded his arms and opened up the folder. "As I noted when you originally hired me, I like to have at least thirty days to do a complete investigation. This allows the opportunity to confirm that the information I've collected is accurate. In your case, we've had a little less than the usual thirty days because this is only a situation where you just wanted proof that your mate is having an affair, and nothing more. Something of that nature is pretty cut and dry."

He began going through the folder, laying out photos to corroborate everything he was telling me.

"I followed Parlay to several celebrity entertainment events, business meetings, and several nights out with the fellas. Although you may have expected differently, all of Parlay's trips were legit. There were no secret rendezvous, no orgy after parties, and no groupies waiting outside of his hotel room."

The lecture from the overly cautious investigator was a waste of his breath. I was only interested in one thing—IS

PARLAY CHEATING??????? All that other crap he was talking was for the birds. I didn't care about confirmation, observation, or litigation—just show me the goods.

"Mr. Featherworth, I understand that it's policy to give a brief overview and things, but really, I just need to know what you were able to find out. Do you have pictures or video or something to show me of Parlay caught in the act of cheating on me or something?"

He paused for a moment as if irritated that I had interrupted his routine. He sighed. "Yes, I do." He went to the back of the folder and pulled out a stack of pictures that were wrapped in a rubber band. "These photos were—"

"Just let me have them. I'll ask the questions after I take a look." I grabbed the stack of pictures from his hand.

My body got hot and my heart raced as I observed the photos. The first picture, a side shot, was of Parlay's naked tattooed body. He was grabbing the waist of a firm body that he was pounding from the back.

Picture number two, a shot from the back, was a picture of a pair of hands grabbing Parlay's buttocks tight as he was in the midst of receiving obvious, intense brain.

The pictures went on and on, shot after shot. I was fuming with anger. I placed the pictures down on the table.

The investigator gave me a moment to gather myself before speaking. "Now, would you like to know where each of the photos were taken?"

After fighting back tears and swallowing hard, I said, "Yes, please," unsure if I really wanted to know.

"If you look on the back of each photo there is a number. Here is a sheet that corresponds with each number." He handed me a sheet of paper. "The location, time, and date is noted on each." He then pulled another piece of paper from the file and handed it to me. "Now, if I can just get your signature here . . ." He placed an X over a blank line. "All it states is that I've explained all liability information and my policy in total." He handed me a pen.

Without even looking, I grabbed the pen and signed my name. As far as I knew, I could have been signing my life away.

In a daze, and without saying a word to Mr. Featherworth, I pulled the envelope that held his final payment out of my purse and laid it on the table in front of him. I then got up from the table and headed to my car.

As I drove, things began to set in. I became infuriated as I thought back to how loyal I'd been to Parlay. Then I became even angrier as I realized how stupid I had been. For more than five years I had been in the game. What the fuck made me think I could give it all up for a man? I'd learned one thing from Vegas—when you find something you're good at, do it and do it well. If I'd stuck by that, I wouldn't have been in the predicament that I was in now.

I was damn good at being *a gangster's girl.* So good that I was *married to the game.* So who the fuck gets a divorce when they're happily married? I should have just stuck with what I knew. Maybe engaged in a few indiscretions, but definitely not have gotten an all-out divorce.

Well, one thing was for sure—it wasn't too late to reconcile. Parlay had definitely pulled one on me, and now he had to pay.

I began to put a plan in action. I could tell from the pictures that I could rule out Diamond and Juicy as suspects. I know it had to be someone from his camp. The investigator said all his trips were legit business, so that left his personal assistant, the company secretary, or some new female artist on the label or something. Whoever it was, I would surely find out, and when I did, the bitch better beware because the old *C* is back.

CHAPTER 15

Angel

"Time for some action"

What more could a woman scorned ask for? In my pursuit of revenge against my cheating husband, everything had fallen into place, just as planned. As I sat here at my computer, logging off, preparing to end my workday, I couldn't help thinking about how close Danielle and I had become. I think she'd even consider me a friend.

Danielle introduced me to another side of life. One thing I'd noticed about her—she was out for self. Her priority was to do whatever to make sure she was set for life.

Even though her fiancé was a very successful basketball star, she didn't just sit back and wait on the goods. She wanted her own income. I was sure that had a great deal to do with the story Shawn told me about her. The last thing she probably ever wanted to do was be dependent on a man.

Determination was her first, last, and middle name—nickname too. She was determined to be on top. Not only did she want the best husband, she also wanted the best job, the best car, the best clothes, and the list went on.

After spending only a few times in the same room with both Dario and Danielle, it was clear to see how she'd used poor little Dario as a stepping stone to get her position as partner in the firm.

It's always obvious when two people of the opposite sex in the same room together have had sex with each other; the tension and chemistry is just there. Which means anybody in the office with a *gaydar* would have suspected that Danielle and I had been together as well . . . even though I didn't consider myself gay—I only did what I did with Danielle as part of the plan.

It was more than obvious, though, that in the case of Dario, Danielle's plan backfired on her. Every day Dario gave her a hard time about one thing or the other; probably because she'd cut him off now that she was partner. Now she was no longer underneath him; they were now equals.

Poor Dario was nothing more than tar on the bottom of her shoe, and I bet if he found out how she had used him, he would've found a way to get the other partners to discharge her of her position. At times I was tempted to invite myself to Dario's gathering of jealousy, self-pity, and anger; my cover dish being revenge. But I figured with Richard and Shawn on my team, who needed Dario?

Richard and I had become quite a team. Still focusing on the wedding, Richard and I meet weekly. Taking note to his interest, I slowly changed my style and appearance to his likings. I added long tracks to my hair and began to wear the designer labels that he was so used to buying for, and seeing his women in.

With each outfit, I was sure to wear a plunging neckline, emphasizing my breasts, which Richard tried his best not to admire during each of our meetings. But he couldn't help from keeping his eyes from traveling down from my pretty eyes to my pretty tits.

He noticed when I noticed, and I always blushed, letting him know that his wandering eyes were okay by me.

The more he and I met, the closer and more comfortable he and I became with each other. He started to confide in me, asking for advice on his and Danielle's relationship.

Always giving the worst advice, I suggested that Richard do things to occupy himself and give her space. I suggested to him that he do all the things she hated him to do, like hanging out with his friends and spending time out of town. I told him that she'd end up missing him so much that she'd come to her senses real quick. I convinced Richard that right now Danielle's career and health were most important, and that he should not give her any extra stress or hindrance.

He listened and followed my advice each step of the way.

Planning the wedding right down to the last detail, our plans were almost complete. The wedding was a little more than a month away, and if the two of them made it to that day as a couple, what a beautiful wedding it would be.

Shawn had been patiently waiting for me to get things rolling so that he could make his move. He made it seem detrimental that he get his money from Danielle.

* * *

I equipped Shawn with a few minor threats he could use against Danielle to get his money.

"Tell her that you are going to tell Richard about the debt she owes and her past involvement in the game."

"I don't see that making her sweat none," Shawn said into the phone.

"Then threaten to tell Richard about the details of Danielle's little dinner with me and John." I paused. "On second thought, that might be too much ammo. Threaten to let her little affair with Jonathan come to the light. And threaten to tell me about her affair with my husband." I figured that would be enough to get her a little nervous.

"All right. But I ain't no man of idle threats, so we need to come with the real—fuck all the foreplay."

"Oh, don't you worry, Shawn. The best is yet to come," I said before ending the call.

Now that things were finally falling right in order, it was time to execute. It was time for little Miss Danielle's world to crumble. It was time I take the same attitude as Danielle—it was time for Angel to look out for Angel.

With that attitude and the motivation from Danielle's deceit and Jonathan's lack of remorse, I was on my way to the ultimate revenge and a new self-image.

As I left the office, I went to go tell Danielle to have a good evening, but she was still in depositions, which she had been in all day. So I headed on out of the office and drove home.

After arriving home, I walked up to the front door. I took a deep breath and then exhaled. I put the key in the lock and went inside. Closing the door behind me, I headed straight to the living room, where I knew John would be sitting, watching the evening news.

"We need to talk," I said right away.

"What's up, honey?" John stood up from his chair to make his way over to greet me with a kiss.

I put my hand up to stop him in his tracks. "It's over," I simply said.

"Excuse me?"

"It's over, Jonathan. I'm not happy in this relationship. You don't treat me the way you should. I deserve better; I'm just settling by being with you."

"Angel, where is all of this coming from? Listen to yourself. Do you know what you are saying? This is crazy." John headed toward me.

"I know exactly what I am saying, and I mean every word—it is over, and I want you out now."

"Don't do this," John responded in an unusual tone.

"It's over, John. It's over." I walked away.

Before turning my back on John, I saw fire in his eyes. I could hear his footsteps behind me, coming towards me.

"Angel, don't walk away from me," he called from behind me.

I ignored him.

"Don't make me do this, Angel." He grabbed me by my shoulder, his teeth clenched.

I jerked around, pulling my shoulder away from his hand, only to find it around my throat.

"Damn it, Angel, listen to me!"

"Get off of me. Let me go," I yelled as I hit him, begging for mercy.

"You are not going anywhere. We've been together too long. I won't let you go."

Shockingly, John threw me to the floor. In all our years of marriage, he'd never laid a violent hand on me. Scrambling to get away from the raging bull now coming towards me, I crawled into the guest bathroom.

When he tried to grab me, I kicked at him and got up and ran into the guest bath.

"Go away. Just leave me alone. It's over. Just leave, John," I shouted through the bathroom door, tears flooding my eyes.

"Open the door." John kicked the door. "Open the fucking door, Angel." He kicked it again.

For a moment there was complete silence.

Boom! The bathroom door came crashing in and hung on its hinges.

John stood there looking like a mad man.

Smack, smack, smack! He hit me repeatedly in my face.

I struggled to my feet and ran to the kitchen and grabbed the cordless phone off its base. Even with him yanking at me and hitting me, I was able to dial 911.

"Help me please—my husband is trying to kill me," I screamed into the receiver, pretending to talk to the police.

Although I had dialed 911, I pushed the flash button to hang up the phone before the operator could answer.

"No need to call the police." John released me. "I'll be gone before they get here."

He walked over to the utility closet, grabbed a garbage bag from it, then headed to the bedroom.

"You ain't even gotta tell me what the fuck is going on," he yelled. "I knew it was pussy you loved. All that bullshit you spoke about making me happy, I knew from the day you mentioned a threesome, it was all for you."

I heard things slamming and crashing.

"So what—you love the pussy that much that you're leaving me for Danielle? Well guess what, Angel—I've been fucking Danielle for months now. That little threesome—that wasn't a first for me to be all up in that. Couldn't you tell how perfectly my dick fit inside her?—So how do you like that?—Fuck you, Angel—Fuck you and Danielle." He walked out of the living room and to the front door with a garbage bag full of clothes and shoes.

Once I heard the front door slam, I exhaled and hung the phone back on the receiver. I then ran to the front door. I peeped out before opening the front door to make sure that John had driven off. I then opened the door and locked the security storm door. I locked the big door and placed the chain on it.

Then turned around and put my back up against the door.

Tears flowed as I slid down the door. The words Jonathan had yelled at me before leaving had pierced my heart.

I knew all along about him and Danielle, but to hear it come from the horse's mouth just brought on a new pain. He said those words to me like I wasn't shit, like I'd meant nothing to him all along.

I sobbed hysterically as the reality of what had just happened set in. It was really over between John and me.

After what seemed like hours of crying, I gathered myself and went to the master bathroom to take a hot shower. I took off all my clothes. I then walked over to the mirror and examined my bruised body and swollen face. My hair stood on my head in every direction. My eyes were red and swollen from crying. I wondered if there was any hope after this.

Spirits low and unsure what to do next, I was ready to give up on my plot of revenge. I had no more energy or fight in me. I was tired, hurt, and drained.

I hopped in the hot shower hoping for some sort of relief.

After getting out of the shower, much calmer and relaxed, I began to straighten up the mess made from the struggle with John, and from his just throwing shit around. Even though his concept of why I was leaving his ass couldn't be further from the truth, I still couldn't figure out why he was in such a rage. Hell, even if I did want to fuck Danielle instead of him, it wasn't like he himself hadn't been fucking her all along anyway.

As I cleaned up the house, I tried to think things through. I decided that it was best to put all this behind me. I had to let it go and move on. I went into the bedroom and gathered any memories or connections I had to Danielle. I gathered the pornographic home DVD we'd made the night of our threesome, the copy of the condo key, and the letter she'd written—the ménage à trois contract.

I placed all these things in a bag and got in my car. Unsure where I was headed, I just began to drive. I drove looking for the perfect place to just toss the items out. Once they were gone, so would the memories.

I don't know if it was fate or woman's intuition, but I ended up near Jonathan and Danielle's secret love nest. I drove cautiously as I entered the neighborhood. Since I had kicked John out, I was sure that this was where he would more than likely go. What I didn't expect was to see Danielle's car parked in the driveway behind his.

As quick as an adrenaline rush, all the aggression from before hit me. I sat and focused on pacing my breathing so I wouldn't do anything stupid.

Instead of running up in there and going crazy, I just drove away. I drove as fast as I could to get out of the area. I knew that if I stayed there any longer, I may have done something I'd regret.

In five minutes flat I was home.

I drug myself into the house and made my way into the kitchen. I poured myself a glass of wine and turned on the TV. I thought to myself, *Sure I had decided to leave John, but I refuse to let that bitch, Danielle, win.*

The game was back on and poppin'. There was no turning back now. I took the final sip of my wine then lay down to sleep. I had a big day ahead of me.

* * *

The next morning I woke up before the alarm clock even went off. I took my time getting dressed, had a hearty breakfast, and headed in to work like every morning.

"Good morning, Danielle." I walked in and sat right down at my desk.

"Hey, girl," she said all perky, as if John hadn't told her about our altercation and the little secret he had shared with me about their affair. "I'm glad you're a little early. I have this big meeting this afternoon. Of course, Dario failed to tell me until last minute, and I need to prepare for it."

"Oh, you know I got your back."

"I know—which reminds me . . . we really need to talk."

"What's up?" I thought to myself. *I know this bitch doesn't have the nerve to try to get me to bail her ass out of a bind and then open up and discuss the issue of her sleeping with my husband.*

"Well, I was hoping we could chat over lunch or something," she proposed.

Not sure if I could contain myself over lunch or even be around her more than thirty minutes straight, I pressured her to talk to me now.

"Girl, you know it's gonna eat me up if you don't talk to me now."

"Okay, but we gotta make this quick," she said. "Step into my office."

I followed Danielle into her office, anticipating what was so important that she needed to tell me.

"Well, this is quite awkward for me, but it's been on my conscience for some time now."

She sat down on a corner of her desk. I stood by the door.

"I really would have preferred for us to have this conversation outside of the workplace, where we had ample time and privacy, but I feel like the longer I wait, the more it's gonna eat me up inside."

She took a deep breath and then walked over to the window. She stared out of it for a moment. Then she turned her attention back towards me. "Well, we've grown very close in such a short period of time, and I feel like I've known you for years. You're like a best friend that I've never had. And it's only right if I come out and tell you the truth." Danielle sighed and grabbed my hands.

I wasn't sure if this was to keep me from hitting her, or if it was for consoling purposes, but either way, I was prepared for the worst.

"Angel, Jonathan and I had relations prior to our ménage à trois, and I'll understand if you no longer—"

"SSSSShhhhhh—Say no more, Danielle. I know all about it." I knew damn well that she knew I knew all about it as well. There's no way John didn't mention his little slip of the tongue to her.

"Last night I realized that John and I could no longer be together. I told him that I was leaving him, and in the middle of our argument, he told me all about the affair you all had."

I put my head down momentarily and then looked back up at Danielle. "Now I have a confession—I'm in love with you. I am willing to put all this behind us and start new, just me and you."

Danielle looked up at me speechless.

"Last night John and I had a huge fight, and he beat me. He actually put his hands on me, Danielle." I started to cry. "He had an anger I'd never seen before. I mean, you should have seen the look in his eyes. He shouted things about me loving the sexual experience you and I had, and he was right—I did enjoy it, and I want to continue to have it."

"I don't know what to say. This is all just too much, too fast," she said as she began to pace.

Danielle looked even more shocked. If I could have captured the confused look on her face I would have bottled it up. It was priceless watching her expression as the affair from hell unveiled itself.

"*Knock! Knock!*" Our conversation was interrupted by a knock at the door.

"Come in," Danielle shouted.

Dario walked into the office as I wiped my tears away.

"Look, Danielle, I talk to you later," I said as I made a quick exit out of her office, leaving the two of them alone.

At my desk I prepared the files Danielle needed for her meeting. Intentionally, I left out important information and only compiled notes that were basically useless, some stats that pertained to an entirely different case altogether.

Pretending to be busy, I buzzed Danielle, who was still in the office with Dario. I wouldn't have been surprised if she was sucking him off every now and then just to keep him quiet.

"Yes, Angel," she answered. I could tell she was on the speakerphone,

"I was just wondering if I should clear your schedule from lunch through the end of the day, since you have this big meeting.'

"Oh, yes please. Thank you."

I waited for her to disconnect the call. Danielle had a bad habit of not releasing the call when she was on speakerphone. And like always, this was one time she didn't disconnect.

I listened as she and Dario chatted.

As usual, Dario was complaining. He wanted more between them. He missed her. He was starting to feel as though she had used him, blah, blah, blah.

After a while, I was bored listening to him complaining and begging. Just as I was about to disconnect the call, it dawned on me that I could use this to my advantage. I pressed the conference call button and called my extension, which of course went straight to voice mail, where I recorded the entire conversation.

The afternoon rolled around quickly.

As Danielle darted out of her office and headed towards the conference room, I handed her the file I had put together for her, and sent her into her meeting poorly equipped. She was heading to a gunfight with a knife.

I couldn't wait for that meeting to end. I didn't even go to lunch.

At around three o'clock that afternoon, Danielle came storming by, signaling with a nod for me to come into her office. She tossed the file on her desk. "What happened here, Angel?"

"What do you mean?"

"This file is missing so much pertinent information. I had none of the information I needed in order to present a complete overview to the staff.

"There was some stuff in here that wasn't relevant to this file at all. I found myself rambling on and on about something totally off base."

"I'm sorry, Danielle. My mind has really been gone this morning. I've just been through so much. I'm torn between my feelings for you and the hurt I feel. I mean, the fight with John last night was a bit much, and then the thought of you all being together is really starting to get to me," I said, fishing for pity.

"I understand," Danielle sighed, really wanting to rip my head off. "What more could I expect?" She flopped down in her chair. "Look, I know the guys are going to be calling me in for a meeting any minute now to discuss what happened today in that meeting. I probably won't be needing you anymore today anyhow, so why don't you take the rest of the day off to get yourself together? Take a couple of days off, if need be."

I walked over to Danielle and hugged her compassionately. I rubbed her back then brought my hands up to her breasts and massaged them.

She threw her head back in pleasure.

I gently grabbed her by her neck and placed my tongue in her mouth, kissing her passionately.

"I'm sorry about the mess-up today. I know what you really want to do is let me go permanently and I understand. But I'd rather have you than this job. So to make this a lot easier for you, for the both of us, I will not be returning."

Her lack of eagerness to try to change my mind let me know that she really did want to fire me, but she felt so guilty that she couldn't. I had given her an easy out . . . for now.

"Think about everything I've said to you today about how I feel about you. You might be letting me walk away from this job, but I hope you decide not to walk away from me and give us a chance." I gave her one last peck on the lips and then walked over to the door. "Please make the right decision," I said as I exited her office.

I returned to my desk and started cleaning things out completely. I had already retrieved a box to put my things in. Once I was all packed up, I retrieved the previously recorded message from my voice mail. I forwarded the message to the other two senior partners, but not before first recording an introductory message of my own.

"This is a conversation that I overheard," I spoke into the phone receiver. "Wishing to stay anonymous, I will just forward it to you all for review. Taking all the company policies and guidelines into consideration, I am sure this is a matter that you all would like to be aware of."

My work here was definitely done. I picked up my box and headed out to my car.

I called Shawn on my way out.

"What's up, Angel?"

"Nothing much. I've started to put things into action; now it's your turn."

"Dat's what's up. Where do I need to step in?"

"Well, I have a few things that you could definitely use to your advantage."

"Oh yeah?"

"Yep. I have these pictures that you won't believe, and a letter to go with it. You call up Miss Home-wrecker and tell her that you have these things, and trust me, she'll give you whatever you want to keep you from wrecking her home."

" 'Nuff talk—Where you want to meet?"

I made arrangements to meet Shawn, and gave him the letter and a copy of the pictures I'd edited perfectly from the DVD. I'd made sure my face was cropped out of each photo. I was sure he knew exactly what to do with it.

I then called Richard and confirmed our weekend meeting to go over some final stages of the wedding planning.

Pleased with the little destruction I'd already caused by popping off a couple of firecrackers, I headed home. Now I looked forward to the big boom.

CHAPTER 16

Jonathan

"True colors"

"*Bang, bang, bang, bang!*" I woke to the sound of someone banging on the door.

I rubbed my eyes and headed to the front door. I opened the door to a crying Danielle.

"I have to end this. We can no longer deal with each other. It's karma. Bad things are happening because of the affair you and I had," she cried hysterically, forcing a number of papers in my face.

I looked at the paper and read the title that appeared on her company letterhead: "Discharge of Commitment of Duties." No explanation was needed there. Danielle had been fired.

"What happened, Danielle? You can't honestly think you got fired because you had an affair with me?" I laughed at the thought.

"This is not a joke!" she shouted.

"Danielle, what you are saying is crazy. I know you're

upset because you lost your job, but I'm sure there is a logical reason, and it's not karma," I assured her.

"We never should have had an affair. We never should have had a threesome—this is all your fault!"

I couldn't believe Danielle was actually blaming me for her loss. "Maybe you lost your job because you were screwing the partner—Did you ever think of that? I can predict how things happened. You got close to Dario, making him feel like you actually had a little bit of interest in him, just so you could have his support for next partner. Once you secured your position, you wanted to cut things off, but Dario was not with that. He wanted to continue things and probably wanted to take things to the next—"

"Stop! Shut up! Just shut up!" Danielle screamed.

"The truth hurts, huh?" I said, tired of her pity fit. I'd had enough of Danielle and her selfish ways.

"This is my life, Jonathan. I've worked hard for this," Danielle continued to yell, as though she was the only one who had problems.

"Sure, you lost your job, but they come dime-a-dozen. Have you forgotten that I've lost my wife? You're not the only one who's lost something, Danielle."

My tone was harsher than I typically used with Danielle, but I wasn't trying to hurt her feelings; I was trying to convince her to think of someone other than herself.

"I'm sorry, but partner with the biggest law firm in Atlanta does not come a dime-a-dozen."

"Well, I guess you should have thought about that before you convinced my wife to leave me."

"Excuse me?" Danielle put her hands on her hips.

"Come on, Danielle, I'm not stupid. You think I hadn't noticed how things changed? First, we had a threesome, and you turned my wife out. Then you offered her a job. Then you two started spending more and more time together, and I started hearing less and less from you. Then out of nowhere my wife decided to leave me. I'm sure that's because she loved your pussy more than she loved my dick." I laughed and walked out the room.

"Are you serious? What you are saying is ridiculous." Danielle followed me and kept going on and on.

"What did you expect to gain from Angel? I know you, Danielle—For each person in your life, there is a reward for you that comes out of the relationship. You don't deal with anyone unless you can get something out of them. So what is it? What does Angel have to offer?"

"I can't believe what you are saying. You have really surprised me. First you're hitting women, and now this."

Ignoring Danielle's wife-beater insinuation and focusing on the situation at hand, I decided to break things down to her.

"Okay, Danielle, you are obviously in denial, so here it is, straight and forward—Let's start with Richard—Poor Richard has no idea that you are only interested in him because he's a husband that can provide a more-than-stable income for you. He's nothing more than a security blanket that you can't wait to spread out and get all wrapped up in. He's a perfect kickstand for times like this—you falling off your bike that you've been riding at the firm.

"Then Dario—poor Dario—was nothing more than a crutch to get your position as partner. Then me, I couldn't provide you with anything material, other than a few pieces of clothing. But you needed me for that attention, affection, and a listening ear that no one else provided. Now Angel, I can't figure out for the life of me, what you needed from Angel—Was it pussy? What was it, Danielle, help—"

Smack!

I was interrupted mid-sentence by a slap to the face.

I grabbed Danielle by the wrist. "I think it's time you leave," I said through my clenched teeth.

Danielle snatched her wrist from my grip, grabbed her things, and stomped out the door, slamming it behind her.

These bitches were really tripping. I didn't know if it was a full moon, something in the water or what, but I'd had enough of females to last me a lifetime. Whoever the fuck made up that saying that you can't live without them must have been lying just to get some pussy.

CHAPTER 17

Danielle

"The walls are crumbling"

I could have sworn someone had cast an evil voodoo spell on me. Any and everything that could have gone wrong, had gone wrong. First I got caught up in a crazy love triangle between Jonathan and his wife, causing me to lose a friend and assistant, my job, and now I was on the verge of losing my man.

Every time my phone rang I damn near jumped out of my skin, because Shawn had been calling my phone, constantly making all sorts of threats about how he was going to ruin my life. He claimed that he knew about me cheating with Jonathan and Dario, and said that he planned to tell Richard.

Although I didn't think he'd really take it that far, I was in no position to take any chances. Right now Richard, and a healthy savings account, were the only things I had left.

Unsure if Shawn had really gone through with things, I decided to give Richard a call and feel him out.

"Hi, honey," I sang as soon as he answered the phone.

"What's up?" he said with little emotion.

"Nothing much. Just thinking about you. How are things going with the wedding planning? Now that I'm no longer working, I have a little time on my hands. Maybe I can help out." I was hoping Richard would be thrilled. "Besides, I wouldn't mind meeting this wedding planner that has helped you to plan my dream wedding."

"Nah, baby, that's quite all right. I'm doing a pretty good job handling this on my own. All I need you to do is rest up for these last couple of weeks. Our wedding is right around the corner," Richard said, politely denying my offer.

"Okay, well, good luck on your game tonight. Will you be coming home this weekend?" I asked, hoping to see my man.

"Yeah, I'll be there. I have a couple of last-minute things to wrap up with the wedding planner."

Lately all I'd heard from Richard was "wedding planner this and wedding planner that," but I guess I should've been happy. Not many women could say their fiancé planned the entire wedding.

My phone began to beep, so I quickly wrapped up my conversation with Richard. "All right, sweetie. Well, call me when you get into town."

"Will do," he said as he hung up the phone.

I clicked over to my other line. "Hello," I said in my most annoyed tone, aware that it was Shawn on the other end.

"Time is ticking, Danielle. Maybe you think this is a game, but it's not. I've given you one too many chances.

This is it, shortie—Either come up off my loot, or you're gonna be very sorry."

I could tell Shawn was no longer playing with me. His tone was more stern and threatening than ever. Still I had no intention of giving him all of his money back, especially when I didn't know my fate. I needed every last dime I came across.

"Okay, Shawn, let's make a deal—I'll give you ten thousand now and a little more in a couple of weeks. As I'm sure you know, I am not working right now and I have a wedding coming up, so my money is kind of tight right now."

"Cool."

I made arrangements to meet Shawn and gave him the money as I promised. I figured that would hold him at least until the wedding. If I could just have until then, that was long enough to keep him at bay.

Once Richard and I said, "I do," everything would fall into place. As Mrs. Richard Anderson I planned to move from Atlanta to Houston, where my future husband spent most of his time. Hopefully, this time I'd pull a disappearing act that not even Shawn could figure out.

Confident that Shawn hadn't ruined my future marriage, I could finally relax and devise a new plan for success. My first move was to secure my marriage and relocate. Once I got to Houston, I'd use my status as the wife of an NBA star, the one and only Richard Anderson, to secure a job at a well-known law firm in the city.

Satisfied with my preliminary plans, I decided to watch a little television. As I sat on the couch and flipped through the channels of the plasma TV, Angel came across my mind. Ever since she had resigned a few days ago, I hadn't spoken to her.

I picked up my cell phone and gave her a call.

"Hello?" she said in a sleepy voice.

"Hi, Angel. It's Danielle," I said softly. "If this is a bad time—"

"No, no, it's fine."

"I just wanted to give you a call since we hadn't spoken in a few days. How is everything?" I asked, sincerely concerned about her well-being.

"I'm making it. I haven't spoken to John, but I've been working on a big wedding and it's kept me pretty occupied."

"Great! I'm glad things are working out for you. Things haven't been as rosy for me, though. I lost my job at the firm."

"Oh my God! What happened? I'm so sorry to hear that, Danielle."

"Somehow, the senior partners found out about a little relationship I was having on the side with one of the partners. But the funny thing is, they only fired me and not him. Deep inside—and it wouldn't surprise me—but I feel like he might have had something to do with it. I mean, it just so happens that as soon as he and I had a deep conversation about us not having a committed relationship, things went downhill."

"I'm truly sorry. I know how hard you worked for that position and how much it meant to you. You must be devastated. Is there anything I can do to help?"

What a sweet girl! I'd never run into such a nice girl. The more I talked to her, the more guilt I felt. Even though I had completely cut John off, I still constantly felt like I owed her something.

"Why don't you come over? I'll call over the masseuse and chef, and we'll have a day of pampering. I'm sure we both could use it." I knew damn well that I should have been watching every penny, but guilt got the better of me.

Angel happily agreed and headed right over.

CHAPTER 18

Ceazia

"Regretful affair"

With Diamond by my side, we rode through the streets of Atlanta on Parlay's tail, like Thelma and Louise. The pictures were just what I needed to confirm my suspicions that Parlay had a bitch on the side. Now I planned to do a little detective work of my own, and eventually catch him in the act. I was on him like white on rice. I knew tonight would be the night; the night I'd confront him and let him know that I didn't need this shit.

Dressed in all black and loaded with camcorder and gun, I was better prepared than the crazy paparazzi.

We pulled up to a nightclub in the downtown area of Atlanta. I had never been to it before and so I wasn't the least bit familiar with it. It looked as though it was some sort of strip club, but the crowd of people that stood in line seemed sort of odd. They just didn't look like the type of crowd that was typical of the clubs Parlay usually frequented. They were dressed as though they couldn't care less which celebrity popped up on the scene.

Parlay drove straight to the valet.

I fell back and watched as he chitchatted with a couple of folks and then walked right through the front door without a problem.

"All right, girl, you ready?" Diamond rested her hand on mine for support.

She asked as if I knew that we were about to walk in on something that would absolutely devastate me. And maybe we were.

Nonetheless, I had come this far and I wasn't about to turn back now. "Let's do it."

We got out of the car and headed to the back of the line. After about a fifteen-minute wait, Diamond and I were in.

Once inside, I looked around the club. It had a weird vibe to it, like they were in a world of their own, unaffected by anything that might have been going on, on the outside.

The club was split into two areas, a downstairs and an upstairs floor. We went into the first side of the club. There, we saw a number of female strippers on the bar, on stage, and a few giving table dances. Unlike most of the predominantly black strip clubs in the area, this club had all races of women dancing. And just like the women dancing, the crowd had consisted of all races alike.

Once Diamond and I had searched the area well enough to convince ourselves that Parlay wasn't around, we moved to the next room. This room was full of male strippers.

Surely, Parlay wasn't in there, so I walked right back out and headed to the upstairs room.

At the bottom of the stairs stood a bouncer. "Is your name on the list? . . . Because that area is reserved for a private party."

"Oh, I'm with Parlay's group," I said, certain his name was on the VIP list.

The bouncer scanned the list quickly. "No Parlay here, ma'am."

Hoping I could use some of my sex appeal, I flirted a little then took a peep at the list.

"Well, maybe it's just under my name."

"What's your name?"

"My name is Tina," I lied, choosing a name I saw listed on the paper.

"Okay, let's see . . . Tina." The bouncer scanned the list again. "There you are. Tina, plus one," he said, checking me off the list

"I'm Tina, and here's my plus one." I grabbed Diamond by the hand.

She gave the bouncer a flirtatious wave, and we then headed up the stairs to VIP.

Once we were upstairs, things began to get stranger and stranger. All the women seemed to be oversized, overdressed, and wore too much makeup. Everybody was so flamboyant and so over-the-top.

I walked to the bar to get a drink as I scanned the crowd for Parlay.

"What cha having sweetheart," a deep voice said with a womanly twist.

I turned around to see a RuPaul look-alike like no other. That's when it hit me—We obviously had strolled into a drag queen's party. *No wonder Parlay's name wasn't on the list; no way would he be caught dead up in here.*

Diamond and I both looked at each other at the same time and did everything we could to keep from laughing.

I grabbed Diamond, and we exited the room just as quickly as we had entered it. That little scene was enough for me. I guess my instincts were wrong. There wasn't anything going down at this place that I needed to concern myself with.

We left the club and headed to the car. We pulled out of the parking lot into a line of cars that were all waiting to exit the lot. Horns were blowing and people were yelling at the one car that was holding up the line.

I pulled around too, so that I could take a look at the car. To my surprise, it was Parlay.

I pulled back into a parking spot to be sure that he couldn't see me. Then I called his phone.

"What up?"

"Hey, honey. What are you doing?"

"Nothing. Chilling. Just leaving the club."

"You on your way home?"

"Nah. So you probably should stay at your crib tonight. I'ma bring some of the fellas over. We got a new artist, and we trying to break him in, you know, sort of like an initiation."

"Oh, okay."

Normally I would think nothing of that, but since I knew that he was cheating on me, I had to use this to my advantage.

I rushed to Parlay's house. I knew he and his entourage wouldn't come in until late. That gave me just enough time to go to the house and set some things up before he arrived.

Using the "Private I" equipment I had gathered, I set up a hidden recording device in Parlay's bedroom as well as the two guest bedrooms. If any action was going down, I would definitely catch it on camera.

Satisfied with my surveillance set-up, I left, and Diamond and I went to my crib for the night.

The next morning I woke up eager to find out just what had gone down at Parlay's house the night before.

I jumped up out of bed and took a quick wash up. I got dressed and then dropped Diamond off at home. Her assistance was no longer needed. I was certain I could handle the rest by myself.

"If you need me," Diamond said as she exited the car, "you know I'm just a phone call away." She winked and walked away.

I smiled, finding comfort in the fact that for the first time in a long time, I just might have met someone who actually did have my back.

After watching Diamond walk up her walkway and get

into the house safe and sound, I then headed straight to Parlay's place.

I pulled up to the house and saw that both his car and his manager's car were in the driveway. No matter what was going on, Parlay's manager, Hakim, was always at his side. Talk about someone having somebody's back; Hakim definitely had Parlay's back.

I wouldn't be surprised if he was the one who had arranged every booty call Parlay had ever had, handpicking the women of Parlay's preference and everything.

"Good morning," I sang as I entered the house.

No one personally greeted me, but the alarm system did when it sounded. "Front door ajar," the automated voice stated, indicating that I had entered through the front door.

After disarming the alarm, I began to look around the house. Surprisingly, it was pretty clean for a bunch of fellas to have occupied it the night before.

"Don't look like much of a party went on here."

I walked to Parlay's bedroom. First, I put my ear up against the closed door and heard nothing. Next, I slowly opened it, only to see Parlay's head sticking out from the covers that wrapped his body. He was sound asleep.

But not for long. I tiptoed over to the window.

"Rise and shine, sweetie." I opened the curtains and blinds, allowing the sunlight to shine right into his crusted eyes.

"Uuuummmmm. Close the blinds, C," Parlay grunted.

"Get up, baby. I have the cleaning service coming in today," I lied.

"Damn, Ceazia!" He threw back the covers and sat up in the bed. He wiped his eyes and then sat there for a minute and yawned.

"Come on, sleepyhead. Get it moving." I clapped my hands to hurry him on.

Parlay stood up and stretched. "Damn, girl." He rolled his eyes at me as he climbed out of bed and headed for the bathroom.

I stood there listening as he closed the door behind him. I heard him pee and then flush the toilet. Next, I heard him turn the shower on.

"Bingo!" I said under my breath.

I ran and gathered up all of the surveillance equipment. I started with his room and then headed to the first guest room to retrieve the equipment from there.

I then headed towards the second guest room. When I entered through the door, I was met by Hakim.

Shit! I forgot about his ass.

"Damn! You could have at least warned a nigga." He walked out of the room ass naked, brushing by me and nudging me on the shoulder.

"Sorry," I yelled back with an attitude. I turned my nose up and walked away.

Just then the alarm clock started to go off.

And besides, what in the hell is he doing walking out the bedroom ass naked anyway? I figured he was still drunk.

It didn't take Parlay any time to get dressed and head out the door. Like every Sunday morning, he was headed to the gym.

As soon as he left, I began reviewing the video. As I suspected, Parlay was up to no good. As everything that was going down on the videotape started to really set in, I almost threw up at the events I was witnessing.

I stopped the recorder, hit rewind, and watched it again. I stood in complete silence with no emotion as I re-watched the footage, praying that my eyes were deceiving me. It couldn't be true.

"Anything but this, God," I prayed. I closed my eyes, rubbed them, and opened them again to see if the image would change. Despite all my efforts, what I was looking at did not change.

"Nooooooooooooo! God, noooooooo," I screamed and ran through the house.

I had no idea where I was running to. I just ran and ran through the house in hopes to get away from that haunting image.

I ran up the stairs, stumbling near the top. There, I just lay and sobbed. "Why, God? Why?" I asked over and over.

Ring ring!

"Hello," I said, sobbing.

"Oh, baby, you don't have to tell me," Diamond said. "The video wasn't good?"

I spent the next hour telling Diamond about the video.

She provided well-needed support. Because of her, I was able to get myself together and come up with a plan of revenge.

Before long, the hurt and great disappointment I'd felt

had turned into a great anger that motivated me to do the ultimate with no remorse.

From this point on, it was straight gangster. I started with the media. I called the radio stations and started the rumor. Remaining anonymous, I told them what I'd discovered and told them I had proof.

Then I hit the Internet, starting with myspace.com, BET, MTV, and any other message board I could get to, I spread the rumor. I even posted pictures and put a snippet of the DVD on sale through Internet purchase.

By the end of the night, I'd spread my discovery all over the United States.

I packed up all my things and cleaned out Parlay's safe. Then I headed back to my condo, where Diamond met me.

I knew it wouldn't be long before Parlay would be contacting me, and it would be war. Although I was always victorious when it came to war, this was just not a battle I was willing to fight.

I made arrangements to have my things packed up and I was headed out.

Amazingly, leaving Diamond was the hardest part. We'd grown closer than I had ever expected over the past month.

Not willing to let me go, Diamond decided to roll with me. Off to Virginia the two of us were headed. Diamond had gone from suspect to "ride or die."

Once in VA, it was back to the old stomping grounds. I had a new outlook on life and a new attitude. With that in mind, I headed straight to Dee-Dee at Creative Styles for a new hairstyle to go with my new attitude.

Surprised to see me, I received service as soon as I walked in. It was great to be back in the old neighborhood. Still up to the same old antics, the shop hadn't changed a bit.

"What chu having?—You know the drill. We still work the same way around here, lil' *durty*." The assistant poked fun at the slight Southern accent I had picked up during my short stay in Atlanta.

I sat in the chair and stared at myself for a minute.

At that moment, so much of my life flashed before my eyes. I thought about all I had gone through in order to survive. I thought back to my past of escorting and stripping, and it just made me sick. A girl shouldn't have to stoop to just any old thing to show that she can take care of herself. But it's amazing how far a pair of long legs and long hair will get you.

It was time for a change; a real change this time.

I turned my head to the left and then the right, admiring myself. Then I decided exactly what I wanted done. "Cut it all off," I said, shocking everyone. "Not just a trim, not just split ends, it all must go."

It seemed as though the entire shop got quiet.

Dee-Dee said, "What?"

"Cut it all off."

"Are you sure? . . . Because once it's gone, boo-boo—"

"I'm sure."

Dee-Dee shot me a look to let me know that it was about to be on and poppin'.

I shot her back a look as if to say, "What are you waiting for?"

Dee-Dee grabbed a clump of my hair and chopped it off. "Well, there is no going back now." She laughed.

"That's cool. Give me a Mohawk," I said, confident with my decision.

Diamond, along with every one else in the shop sat in disbelief as Dee-Dee cut my signature look—long, black hair—down to a couple of inches.

A couple of hours and a new hairdo later, I was out the beauty shop and on to the tattoo shop. I went out on a limb. I walked in the shop and chose a tribal tattoo.

"I'll take this from the beginning of my ass crack all the way up my spine and to my neck," I said, again shocking everybody in the shop.

"That's gonna be painful," a woman said.

"Is this your first tattoo?" the artist asked.

"Yes, it is."

"You sure—"

"Yes, I am."

"Okay, let's do it."

Another two hours and four hundred dollars later, I was out the shop. I'd had a full day.

We headed to the oceanfront and got a cozy little hotel room.

Avoiding certain areas because of my haunting past, I went for something a little less extravagant than usual.

Laying down all my past behind me, I lay down to sleep. I knew the game was a permanent part of my life and was hoping to play it differently.

CHAPTER 19

“Richard”

“Party over”

"What a fucking night!" I mumbled as I grabbed my bags and headed out the locker-room after the game.

"Anderson! Anderson!" a fan shouted as I exited.

I turned to see a thugged-out fella standing in the cut. Unsure if this nigga wanted to rob me or had beef, I kept walking. He just didn't look like an autograph seeker.

"Yo, son, I think you may want to hear this," he continued to yell and walk towards me.

I really wasn't for the bullshit. Something just didn't feel right about ol' dude. I'd had heard plenty of stories about players in this same type of scenario where they think they're just about to hook up a fan with an autograph, but end up checking in all they shit.

I tried to ignore him and kept walking.

"I'm trying to holla at you about your wifey, Danielle," he shouted.

Hearing Danielle's name certainly gained my attention. I had to stop at that point. "What's up, man?" I dropped my bag on the floor, just in case I had to go toe-to-toe with this nigga.

"Yo, kid, I ain't got no beef. I'm just trying to hand you these. It's just a little something you may want to look at before you get married next week." He handed me an envelope then walked off.

Curious as to what was in the envelope, and even more concerned with my safety, I threw the envelope in my bag and decided to take a look later.

A few steps later, I was out the stadium and in my car. From the relative safety of my car, I decided to take a look. I wondered what was so important that this nigga went through so much to get it to me. Everything, from anthrax to hate mail, ran through my head as I opened the envelope.

"Pictures," I said to myself. I pulled out the photos backwards and flipped them over—There was my wife-to-be giving some nigga good head.

I continued to flip through the photos. My wife was in every position imaginable, doing tricks I hadn't even seen—with a woman.

All sorts of emotions ran through my mind as I sat in my car dumbstruck. *I should call this bitch and check her trifling ass. Better yet, I shouldn't even go home. I should just get with one of these groupies and bring her to the crib, then kick Danielle's 'ho' ass out and humiliate the fuck out of her.*

Although I wasn't sure how to handle things with

Danielle, I was sure about one thing—the wedding was off. There was no way she could talk her way out of this one.

I wasted no time calling Angel.

"Hello?" Angel answered in a sleepy tone, making me aware of the time.

I was so wrapped up in the moment that I didn't even realize it was after 11:00 p.m. on the West Coast, which meant it was after 2:00 a.m. in Atlanta.

"I'm so sorry for calling so late, Angel. No disrespect."

"It's okay. What's wrong? I can tell from the sound of your voice, there is a problem."

"Damn! It's that bad, huh?—This bitch really got me fucked up," I said, embarrassed that Angel could hear the pain in my voice.

"Oh no. It's Danielle. What happened, Richard?"

"The wedding's off, Angel."

"No, Richard, we can work this out. The wedding is next week."

"Nah, shortie, it's a wrap."

"Are you still coming here tomorrow?" Angel asked.

"I dunno."

"Please still come. We can have lunch and talk about things. Maybe it's not as bad as it seems. Sleep on it and we'll talk tomorrow."

Wanting to have someone to discuss Danielle's deceit, I agreed to meet with Angel the next day.

* * *

Normally I never participated in the after-game gatherings, but tonight I refused to return to a lonely hotel room and wallow in pity. I couldn't believe that bitch could be so dirty.

I called up my homeboy to see where niggas was hanging for the night. Not many people were out, but a few of the fellas were at one of the local strip clubs.

As crazy as it might seem, I'd never gone to a strip club before, so this was my first. I had no idea what to expect; I'd only heard stories.

I pulled up to valet, took a deep breath, and headed inside. I spotted my boys right away.

Excited to see me out, they called over every top-notch chick in the place. I had lap dance after lap dance and bottled water after bottled water, since I was never one to drink.

A gallon of water and a hundred chicks later, I was ready to roll. I hollered at my boys and headed to the hotel, checking my phone on the way.

I had five missed calls and three messages, all from Danielle. That was odd. Danielle was never the type to blow a nigga up. It was as though she knew what was up or something.

Refusing to call her back, but interested in what she had to say, I listened to the messages:

Beep—Hey, baby. Great game tonight. Give me a call.

Beep—Richard, I've called you several times, and you won't answer. I hope everything is okay. Give me a call.

Beep—Okay, this is ridiculous and not like you. What is going on? I'm going to sleep. I'll see you tomorrow. I hope you have a good excuse.

I laughed at the thought of this bitch actually having an attitude with me, and here I was holding pictures of her fucking some dude and a chick—Now, that's funny.

The next morning I woke up refreshed and eager to get back to Atlanta.

Sleeping the whole flight through, I woke to the voice of the captain, "Flight attendants, prepare for arrival."

Just the words I wanted to hear.

Angel had offered to pick me up from the airport, normally something Danielle would do, but there was no way in hell I was calling that bitch.

I walked up to the car.

"Hi, Richard," she sang.

"What up, Angel? Thanks for picking me up. And you were on the time—That's what's up."

"When have I ever let you down?"

Never.

Sad to say she'd been there more than my own fucking girl. Just thinking about that was making me feel uneasy about the pictures again.

Angel obviously picked up on my change of attitude. "Did I say something wrong?"

"Just a lot on my mind—Where we headed?"

"This little Thai restaurant just outside the city. I figured we needed a small secluded spot."

"Perfect."

When we arrived at the restaurant and got seated, Angel got right down to business. "Okay, what's the deal?—Are we having a wedding or not?"

"Damn! You right to it, huh?"

"No need to sugarcoat—You are a grown-ass man."

I loved her feistiness. She'd been that way since day one and I had loved it ever since.

"What? You want to fight?" I laughed.

"You'll lose." She smiled.

My mind drifted as I gazed into her smile. I never noticed just how pretty her smile was until now.

"Hhhheeeellllloooooo," she sang, "earth to Richard."

I asked like I wasn't daydreaming, "What up?"

"So what's the deal, Richard?—We don't have much time."

"A'ight, Angel, I'm just gonna put it out there—Danielle cheated on me. She had a more-than-freaky threesome, and I've got the pictures to prove it. There is no way out—The wedding is off."

Angel shook her head and put her head down.

"What is it, Angel?"

"Nothing."

"Angel, talk to me."

"I wanted to tell you. I swear, I did."

"Tell me what, Angel? Come on, baby girl, you can talk to me."

"It's just that I feel so bad. I should have told you. I was being so selfish."

"Angel, listen to me"—I grabbed her hands—"whatever it is, you can tell me."

"I have to leave. The wedding is off. I'll send you your termination papers." She got up from the table and walked away.

I threw twenty dollars on the table, which was more than enough for the drinks we'd ordered, then rushed behind her. "Angel, Angel, wait up."

I met her at the car.

She unlocked the door, and I got in.

I didn't say anything. I just rode with her as she drove to nowhere.

Fifteen minutes later, I finally spoke. "Turn there." I pointed to the Grand Hyatt on Peachtree.

She pulled in.

I ran in and got a hotel room and called her in.

We walked to the room in silence.

I opened the door and signaled for her to enter.

"Make yourself comfortable. I come here all the time, when I feel like I just need to get away from the commotion of the world around me."

"Thank you. I feel so bad, Richard. Could you ever forgive me?"

"Forgive you for what? What is it, Angel?" I sat beside her on the bed and placed my arm around her neck, begging her to tell me.

"Richard, I knew. I knew she was cheating on you, but instead of telling you, I encouraged you to give her space. I gave you all the wrong advice. I've done this long enough to know when someone is cheating. I'm sorry."

Angel's tears seemed to carry more pain than just this situation.

"Angel, it's okay. But I know you're not telling me everything. You're carrying something more. I don't know if it's me, or something personal, but I can see you have more pain inside. You want to talk about it?"

She forced out a grin. "You got all night?"

"Yes, I do." I smiled and pinched her cheek playfully.

Angel told me how she'd been married for so many years, and that the man she'd put her all into just turned his back on her one day and began to cheat. So she felt even more guilt because she knew what it was like to be cheated on, and yet she still did nothing when she knew Danielle was cheating on me.

"Angel, it's okay. I don't hold you responsible. I'm just sorry you had such a terrible experience. Your husband had to be crazy to leave such a wonderful woman like you." I hugged her.

"Thank you, Richard." Angel laid her head on my chest and sobbed.

Exhausted from all the events I lay back on the pillows. I pulled Angel beside so her back was on my chest.

I examined Angel. She was beautiful—perfect smile, gorgeous frame, perfect breast, and most importantly, a loyalty like no other.

"Why couldn't you be my Angel?" I pulled her hair back and kissed her on her forehead.

To my surprise, Angel lifted her head and kissed me gently on the lips. Then she kissed me again and again.

I knew exactly what was about to happen, and I wanted it bad. I had no regrets as I removed her clothes piece by piece. It just felt right.

The next morning Angel and I ordered room service and had breakfast in bed.

After breakfast we showered together. Neither of us had any regrets as the day went on.

Noon rolled around quicker than the blink of the eye and it was time to leave.

To avoiding any altercation, I told Angel to go ahead, and I took a car service home.

We'd decided not to the call the wedding off. It was definitely going to be one to remember!

CHAPTER 20

Danielle

"Here comes the bride"

My special day had finally come.

"What a beautiful bride," I said to myself, twirling in the mirror in my ten-thousand-dollar dress.

I made it look every bit worth the money. The beaded pearls that covered the entire top, including the back of the bodice, were hand-sewn. They were beautiful and pure like they'd been removed directly from the oyster and applied to my dress. The sheer sleeves, pearls sewn in the seams, went down my arm and around my wrists, as well as the neck of the dress.

The detachable six-foot train was now gathered and clasped to the back of the dress. But it was the veil that really set things off. (I just happened to have seen it on the cover of *Soap Opera Digest* magazine while standing in line at the grocery store.) The base was nothing but pearls, with layers of sheer made out of the exact material of the sheer on my dress.

The designer who'd made my dress and the veil made an exact replica. I felt like a star about to take a photo shoot for the cover of a magazine.

Richard had really outdone himself. I could just kiss the wedding planner he'd hired to put it all together. I couldn't have done a better job myself.

"It's time," a voice yelled from the other side of the door. It cracked open, and Angel walked in.

"Angel! What a surprise!" I was beyond excited to see her. "I didn't think you would make it."

"Oh, I had to be here for this." She hugged me gently, so as not to mess up my dress or my makeup. She then held both of my hands in hers. "You look sooo beautiful. I knew you, of all people, would have a wedding to remember. This will be the wedding of all weddings. I took a peek around the church before coming up, and the set-up is gorgeous. You really went all out. This wedding will be talked about forever," she said, making me feel real good inside.

"You know I always aim for the best." I smiled. "You should see the layout of the reception. Girl, I'm talking ice sculptures, and we have an awesome dance troupe performing. Are you going to make the reception?"

"If you make it that far." Angel rolled her eyes.

"Excuse me?" I asked, confused by her response and the sudden change in her demeanor.

"I said, 'If you make it that far." She then caught herself and paused.

"I'm sorry. I guess I'm still a little bitter about my divorce from John. Forgive me. This is your day. Enjoy, sweetie." She gave me a hug and made a quick exit, but not before turning to look at me over her shoulder and smile.

I turned and stood to face the mirror.

Just then I heard the music begin to play.

"All right, baby girl," I said to myself, "it's show time."

I rushed to the ballroom door to make my grand entrance. Smiling and walking with my head high, I felt like a queen as I walked down the rose petal-covered aisle.

Richard stood there smiling, as if this were an arranged marriage, and it was his first time seeing his chosen bride.

Once at the altar, I placed my hands into Richard's.

The preacher proceeded with a few words. He then asked the infamous question, "Is there anyone who objects to the marriage?"

I felt as though one of those damn pearls from my gown was stuck in my throat, when I heard Richard begin to speak.

"I would like to make a statement, before we go any further," he said, completing scaring the fuck out of me.

I whispered, "Richard, what the fuck are you doing?"

I smiled to the audience, trying not to seem too rattled.

I silently repented for using such language in a church.

Richard turned his head and nodded to his best man, as if signaling him to do something.

His best man returned the nod and exited the door to his left.

Everyone began whispering and chitchatting. The word *embarrassment* couldn't describe the emotion I was feeling.

A few seconds later, the best man rolled in a film projector. He then nodded to one of the ushers standing at the church doors.

The next thing I know, the lights dimmed, and two screens, one to the left and another to the right, came on. Ordinarily they were used for the congregation to read the words to the songs of praise and worship.

What in the hell!

That familiar pain came back to haunt me. My chest tightened, and my heart began to race. The panic attacks were back. Trying to be a beautiful bride, a very little part of me still hoping for the best, I stood up straight and closed my eyes briefly to try to meditate on something positive, to keep from falling over in a sweat.

All of a sudden, the guests roared with comments and gasps.

When I opened my eyes, I couldn't believe the sight before me.

"Oh my God!" I heard someone say.

"This is crazy!" another voice from the back shouted.

"I have never . . ." an older woman gasped.

I was just as shocked as the guests at what appeared on the screens—clips of me performing every sexual act known to man, and woman for that matter. It was obvious that the pictures were from my threesome with Jonathan and Angel.

I looked over at Richard, who was just standing there shaking his head in disgust.

"Richard, please . . . that isn't me. Someone is trying to

ruin our wedding day." I tried desperately to persuade Richard.

It worked for R. Kelly, so on a wing and a prayer, I was hoping that it would work for me, but Richard didn't budge. It was as though I was talking to a brick wall.

His eyes focused on the screen, Richard didn't even acknowledge me in the least bit.

People began to get up and leave the sanctuary, while the nosier guests stayed to see what would happen next.

"I guess the best still wasn't good enough for you, Danielle." Richard gave me a disgusting look then walked off, leaving me standing there alone at the altar.

Tears rolled from my eyes as the realization set in. "Richard," I yelled out one last time.

From the door, he turned around and looked at me.

"I'm pregnant—I'm having your baby."

I knew if anything could make Richard re-consider, it would be hearing that I was pregnant. I knew how important having a child was to him.

But that wasn't even enough to send him running back down the aisle into my arms to give me one more chance. He shook his head and walked out the door.

The next few weeks were hell for me. I thought I had lived through hell before, but this time, the flames were even hotter and the unbearable heat was suffocating.

I'd fallen into a deep depression. I swear, I just wanted to die. The child growing inside my belly was the only thing that kept me alive; otherwise, I would have committed suicide a long time ago.

I might as well have been dead though. My life was over; I had nothing more to look forward to.

I turned the phones off, cutting off all communication with the world. I hadn't seen outdoors for days. I was completely cut off from the outside world and had no desire to be a part of it. From the hole I had dug for myself and jumped into headfirst, there was no way out. I was in way too deep.

A knock at the door interrupted my daily swim in pity. I drug myself from the bed and opened the door, not even looking through the peephole. Hell, at this point I could only hope for a crazed murderer to be standing outside my door.

Shawn stood on my doorstep and looked at me like he saw a ghost. "Come on, ma, you can do better than dis."

"Fuck you! If you're here for money, I don't have none. I have no money, no job, no friends, no hope, and no one who even cares!" I said, trying to hide my tears behind the anger.

"I care, baby girl—that's why I'm here."

"No, you don't. You just want your damn money! Fuck you, Shawn. This is all your fault anyway. You did this to me. You gave him those pictures. I know it was you, and don't you dare try to deny it. You ruined my life! You ruined my life, you bastard!" I began hitting him repeatedly in the chest.

He let me get a few licks off then grabbed me by my

wrist. He pushed me back as he came in the door and kicked the door behind him. "Sit down and shut the fuck up." He pushed me down onto the couch.

He examined himself for any bruises or scratches.

"Now, calm your happy ass down. You did this to yo' gotdam self. Look, Danielle, I just came to the *A* to get my loot, but when I got here I saw that I wasn't the only one out for you."

"What do you mean?"

"Dat bitch Angel is the one who set you up. She been plotting on you for the longest, and your dumb ass, so worried about me avenging shit, fell right into her trap. Now I admit, I approached ol' girl just to see where her head was at and shit. I needed to let her know that my vendetta was bigger than hers and that she needed to fall back. But then ol' girl got to talking about how you had ruined her life and shit, and I decided to let her get hers off too, you know, for closure.

"But all that other shit was her idea. She gave me all that stuff—the pictures and everything—and paid me to give it to yo' man. I really wasn't down wit' dat, but I needed my loot so bad, I was down for whatever.

"I hoped dat ten grand would be able to hold shit down for a while, but I owe niggas and they are tired of excuses. I was desperate, ma. It all boils down to this—it's either me or you—I could easily tell them you robbed them and put you under the fire, but I promised to handle things, ya feel me?"

I couldn't believe what Shawn was telling me. I figured

he was under pressure, but I had no idea it was to that level. I respected him for telling me the truth, but I still knew that I had to keep him at arm's length.

"Damn, I had no idea." I got up from the couch and paced. "And just to think that I offered Angel's ass a job, that I actually felt sorry for her. Well, ain't this a bitch? When I thought I had the most game in my little pinky than most did in their whole body, another bitch was running game on me." I laughed. What else could I do?

"So what's the deal, Danielle?—The fact still remains, I need the loot."

Hearing Shawn's words . . . that's when it hit me—I had a little revenge that I owed someone, and with Shawn as an added interest, I just may be able to put things into action.

"Okay, Shawn," I turned and said confidently, "you want your money?—You help me get Ceazia Devereaux, and I will get you every dime, I promise."

" 'Ceazia'? Wifey of the late Vegas?—You still after that bitch?" Shawn laughed, as if to say it was an impossible task.

Now I knew it wasn't an easy feat, or I'd have long had her ass by now. "Yeah—is that a problem?"

"Man, you should have *been* got that bitch. She was right here in the *A* with you. Dat bitch just moved back to VA."

That was all I needed to hear. I had to get out of Atlanta anyway. Now I had a concrete reason and motivation, so why not go back to Virginia and reclaim my home and my money?

"Okay, so let's do it, since it's so simple."

"You ain't said but a word." Shawn erupted in a mischievous grin and extended his hand. "I hope you ready to ride or die, because this shit is 'bout to get real gangsta!"

"I always wanted to be *A Gangster's Girl*." I extended my hand, with a promise to ride or die as we set out on our mission to get Ceazia!